D1095935

WEAVER

by

Tish Thawer

ALP

www.amberleafpublishing.com

www.tishthawer.com

First Edition
First Hardback Printing, 2022
ISBN: 978-1087984537

Cover design by Regina Wamba
Edited by Cassie McCown
Character Illustration by Art by Steffani / Steffani Christensen

Amber Leaf Publishing, Missouri
www.amberleafpublishing.com
www.tishthawer.com

Praise for *Weaver*

"Visually stunning, Thawer's *Weaver* is a fresh YA Fantasy that will capture your heart and convince your mind dreams really do come true."
~ **Award-winning Author, Stacey Rourke**

"Atmospheric. Magical. And swoon worthy. Thawer's YA Fantasy is full of *Practical Magic* vibes and will have you rushing to bed in search of a Weaver of your own."
~ **International Bestselling Author, Belinda Boring**

"Lush and atmospheric, *Weaver* is a beautiful, carefully-crafted YA fantasy."
~ **Casey L. Bond, author of House of Eclipses**

"An illustrious YA Fantasy that blurs the line between dreams and reality, obscuring together two worlds into one visionary romance."
~ **Award-winning Author, Cambria Hebert**

"A beautifully written YA fantasy, wrapped in darkness and love. *Weaver* is full of stunning imagery and unforgettable characters that will keep you turning the pages until morning."
~ **Rebecca L. Garcia, author of Shadow Kissed**

"Spellbinding and packed with mystery and breathtaking landscapes, the world of the Weaver will assuredly enchant you."
~ **Cameo Renae, USA Today Bestselling Author**

Praise for *Guiding Gaia*

"The imagery Thawer developed is amazing. Her love of Gaia radiates from each page of this compelling story I eagerly lost myself in. If you liked *Lore*, this is your next must read!"
~ Award-winning Author, Stacey Rourke

"Guiding Gaia is the story you've been waiting for - beautifully written with twists and turns that keep you addicted, devouring each page until the epic end! This is Tish Thawer at her very best. A must read for 2021!"
~ International Bestselling Author, Belinda Boring

"Thawer brings a breath of fresh air to the genre with this beautifully told story. I love this unique perspective of Gaia, her strengths and her vulnerabilities."
~ Bestselling, Award-winning Author, Kristie Cook

"Guiding Gaia is the book I needed most this year without even knowing it. Tish Thawer has taken the history of this mythos and seamlessly turned it into something unexpected and extraordinary. This is one YA tale you don't want to miss."
~ Paranormal Romance Author, Brynn Myers

Praise for *The Witches of BlackBrook*

"Tish Thawer's intriguing story line is weaved and crafted into a magical and spellbinding web that kept me up until the wee hours of the morning biting my finger nails and cheering for the sisters. Strong story line and well-developed characters that will sweep you away. I was completely floored by this amazing book and I recommend it to everyone!"
~ Voluptuous Book Diva

"Tish Thawer is an amazing wordsmith. I have devoured several books by her and she never disappoints. The blend of history with contemporary is just genius and I can't wait to see what this author will come up with next. Add this to your list as a must-read recommendation from me! An EASY 5 out of 5 stars!"
~ NerdGirl Melanie

"Overall, The Witches of BlackBrook was a grand slam for me. I was so enchanted by this spellbinding tale of hope, love, and a bond that can't be broken. There was something special about it and I honestly think it had something for all different types of readers. Whether you're into romance, historical, paranormal, new adult, etc. the author effortlessly weaves so many elements together to create a flawless experience for whoever picks it up. If you're looking to be enchanted and escape your mind for a couple hours, I highly suggest picking up The Witches of BlackBrook and diving on in!!"
~ Candy of Prisoners of Print

He walked out of my dream, identifying himself only as the Weaver. In a black cloak, with eyes like stars, there was a shimmer to the way he moved. He was beautiful. Ethereal… and I was going to make him mine.

***

Alone for most of her life, Milly is determined to make the man of her dreams a reality. Using her hereditary magic, she sets out on a lifelong quest, entering a world of shadows and secrets. But little does she know, to possess his heart, she'll have to give away her own… for the only way to love a Dream Weaver is to become his Queen of Nightmares.

***

The choice between love and magic is a dangerous thing.

For Dee,
the love of my life and the weaver of my dreams

WEAVER

Roarke – Colorado, 1847

I TILTED MY HEAD TO THE SKY, lifting a hand to block out the blinding light. A torrent of shooting stars streaked across the black expanse, filling it with cosmic rays, practically turning night to day.

"My son, it's you. You've been chosen." My father clapped me on the shoulder.

I looked to my brother, his head hanging in disappointment. The stars were so bright and unnatural. I couldn't deny my father's claim.

"Tonight, as soon as you fall asleep, you'll travel to the gate and receive your powers." He continued.

"What happens after that?" I asked, my voice cracking and unsure.

"Then you'll claim your destiny as the next Weaver."

I shook my head. I spent my entire life waiting for this moment, but now that it was here, I wasn't sure I was ready—wasn't sure I'd *ever* be ready.

I stared at my father as my brother returned to our cabin, my mother's cries spilling out the open door. We both knew what this meant. My father's time as the Weaver was over, and my family would be forced to leave. For only one Weaver could remain hidden here at a time.

"Is there no way you can stay?" My voice hitched.

He met my eyes with tears in his own. "You know we can't. You're a grown man now, and as soon as you receive your powers, your soul will begin searching for your queen." He reached out and pulled me into a hug. "I'm not going to lie, son. It can be a long and lonely endeavor. But promise me you'll never give up hope."

I tightened my hold, not ready to let go.

"I promise."

Milly - Rhode Island, 2016

A BLAZING SUN SCORCHED MY SKIN, baking me in its heat along with the wilted tomatoes dried on the vine. "Mama, what should I do with these?" I yanked the dead plants from the dirt, grasping one in each gloved hand.

"Toss them into the compost. Their demise will soon help provide life for another." She turned to me, smiling and with love in her eyes. "You're doing so well, Milly. The earth has truly responded to your magic this year."

I held my head high, proud to receive my mother's praise as I looked out across the blooming beds of our gardens.

At thirteen, our hereditary magic now flowed through my veins. And thanks to my mother's guidance, I knew this was my calling too. Our souls were connected to this land, and my magic grew stronger with each and every season.

"Milly..." Mother whispered, her voice sounding wrong.

I turned in time to watch her fall.

"Mama!" I raced to her side and grabbed her hand. "Mama, what's wrong?"

"My darling girl. I've taught you everything you need to know. And now it's time for you to be brave. Promise me you'll be brave."

Tears streamed down my cheeks, and I knew this was it. Mama was finally leaving me. After falling sick over the past few years, she made it her mission to teach me all she could about our magic and how to make a living off our land, but I prayed this day would never come.

"Milly, promise me you'll continue your education, and more than anything, promise me you'll follow your heart."

Mama's eyes closed, and something inside me broke. The plants and flowers surrounding us wilted alongside my pain.

"I promise."

1

Present day…

DARKNESS SURROUNDED ME AS I OPENED MY eyes, its emptiness clinging to me like a second skin. A shiver rattled my bones as my feet hit the cold planks of my cottage's hardwood floor. Smoothing my nightgown straight, I walked to my altar, ready for my next attempt.

It had been two days since my last dream, and all I could remember was that I didn't want it to end. I tried to force myself back to sleep—back to *him*. Dark, sparkling eyes from beneath his hood were all I could remember before being ripped awake without warning. Now I was desperate to get back. There was something about him I needed to learn. Something magical calling to my witch's soul.

My last batch of skullcap, rosemary, and mugwort sat cold in my mortar. This time, an added pinch of passionflower should stop my mental chatter. I needed to focus if I was going to make this work.

Three times before, I'd seen him shimmering in the distance, watching me from afar. The most recent dream I recalled was like a fairy tale. With glistening castles and lush forests surrounding me, it was full of mythical creatures who let me frolic alongside them without a care in the world. I spotted him standing behind a stone outbuilding, staring and monitoring my every move.

The dream before that took place in a desert where I lived a fabulous life as the close friend of an important sheik. There he'd been huddled behind a spice cart in the market, but I could still feel his eyes upon me.

Regardless of my dream's location, my watcher was always there. Unfortunately, my last dream had been yanked away, leaving me with a complete void. Something had changed, and I was determined to find out what.

The cold feel of my pestle in hand was a welcome shock to my system. A signal to my body we were about to begin. Grinding herbs was a ritual I cherished.

"Take care now, Milly. Too harsh a stroke and you'll bruise the lavender."

I smiled at the memory.

For six years now, I'd tended the gardens of our humble cottage alone, honing my craft in the Arcadia Forest outside of West Greenwich, Rhode Island. Mother always said it came naturally to me.

Squinting against the dim morning light, I reached above my head and pinched off a sprig of dried passionflower, adding it to my mortar. Now nineteen, book-smart, and full of Mama's wisdom, I rolled my wrist as she taught me, grinding the herbs in a soft motion until the sharp fragrance filled the air.

It was ready.

After setting the kettle on the burner, I bound three pinches of the herbal concoction into a small square of cheesecloth and dropped it in. Once steeped, the elixir should work right away. Within minutes, I'd be back asleep.

Busying myself while the water boiled, I combed my dark-auburn hair straight, then braided it into two plaits and wrapped them into a bun again. Closing my eyes, I could almost see him. *Almost.*

He moved like a wisp of fog through my dreams, seeping in and out of my mind and settling between the cracks of my heart. The dark hood of his cloak was always in place, concealing his features from my view, and only once had I seen his eyes. Like a galaxy of stars contained in a marble, they shimmered from beneath his hood. I held his silver gaze, my magic rising. Then all was lost. The connection slammed shut, jerking me awake as if somehow he kicked me out of my own dream.

But tonight I had a plan.

Instead of experiencing my dream while he waited on the sidelines, I was going to seek him out. Find out if he was real or just a figment of my imagination. I'd had many book boyfriends over the years, but this was different—as if the man of my dreams could somehow be real. And if he was, I wanted to talk to him, ask him questions, and find out exactly who he was. I wanted to know why he continued to appear in my dreams. And, more importantly, how he managed to leave a lasting mark upon my soul. But most of all, I wanted to know what he was about to say the last time we were together, before I'd been ripped away.

I smiled as the kettle whistled. Tonight, it would be me who was stalking him.

Steam swirled around my face as I sipped from the cup. The sharp taste of skullcap, mugwort, and rosemary was still present, softened only by the addition of the passionflower petals. This was the first time I'd used this combination, but I was confident it was going to work. The only concern was how well. Getting lost in a dreamscape could be a dangerous thing.

Raising the carved-wood cup to my lips, I drank and then set my intention.

Lucid dreaming come to me. Find the one that I do seek. Grant me control in this way. Bring me to him on this day.

I relaxed my head into the feather pillow, readying myself for our next encounter.

A bloodred sun blazed behind my closed eyes, my outstretched arms and fingers floating on the surface of the cool water below. A bright blue sky and green leaves welcomed me, mocking the colors of my mismatched eyes. I rose from the rectangular pool filled with the bluest water I'd ever seen and was met with dolomite pillars lining both sides of the space. My eyes followed their structured lines to a square building standing directly ahead. Fountains and flowers trailed down its sides, so beautiful they could rival the Hanging Gardens of Babylon. I looked left and right, trying to spot my watcher, but I didn't see him… *yet*.

Emerging from the pool, I walked up the marble staircase and was met by two young men. Tanned and with gold bracelets encircling their upper arms, they were dressed in nothing more than white loincloths. The first approached, reaching out to drape a white dressing gown over my gold swimsuit, the thin material floating behind me in the warm summer breeze. The other bowed at the waist, keeping his head low as he raised a platter of grapes on outstretched arms. I plucked the fruit from the tray, then followed the cypress-lined walkway up the stairs and through the courtyard, heading straight for the building. Tonight, it seemed, I was in ancient Greece.

Gauze curtains floated around me as I pushed my way through the entrance and into a massive bedroom. My ancient history lessons rushed back to me as I took in the Grecian architecture. More pillars lined the space, and carved bands of Greek reliefs encircled the ceilings. Gold braziers hung from the walls, their charcoal flames

[9]

providing the only light throughout the room. Finally, I noticed an oversize four-poster bed sitting atop a raised dais against the far wall. Its sides were curtained in more of the gauzy material, and lying atop it was a white chiton and a golden crown. I was clearly meant to put them on.

Changing quickly, I slipped the gown over my head, the gold shoulder clasp and laurel headpiece making me feel as if I were somehow important here.

"That's because you *are* important."

There he is.

His deep voice floated from the shadows, sending a chill up my spine. I wondered if he had watched me change.

"It's not polite to spy on a lady."

"It's hard not to when you're all I can see."

Flushed, I placed a hand on my chest and turned to face him.

The room was empty.

"Who are you, and why are you stalking my dreams?" I asked, taking a deep breath.

"Stalking is such a harsh word." His voice again drifted to my ears.

"What else would you call it?" I tilted my head, trying to pinpoint his location.

"Maybe… *enchanting* your dreams."

Before I could utter another word, the ceiling exploded into a thousand stars. Tiny silver lights twinkled against a black expanse, enveloping me as if I were inside the private cosmos of the gods.

"So… are you enchanted?" His voice sounded from directly behind me, his warm, featherlight breath brushing across my skin.

"Yes," I replied. There was no reason to lie.

"Good. Then I'll see you again tomorrow night."

I spun around, desperate to lay eyes on him, but the room was empty once more. "At least tell me who you are," I called out.

From the shadows drifted, "It's time to wake up, Milly."

I woke abruptly, the familiar scent of my cottage permeating the air. Sitting up, I rubbed my chest then startled, wrapping my arms around me as another chill raced up my spine.

Someone was here.

Squinting into the darkness, I caught a shimmer in the shadow across the room and shrank back beneath my wall of blankets, unable to move.

"Don't worry. I've only come to answer your question." His voice was the same but somehow sharper. Clearer. "They call me the Weaver."

The Weaver? I must still be dreaming.

Emboldened more than usual, I slid from my bed and crossed the room. He remained deep within the shadows, his form slowly coming into view.

Broad-shouldered and at least a foot taller, he towered over me. But I wasn't intimidated. I felt safe. Safe enough to lean up on my tiptoes and place my lips against his.

My elixir worked. I was in control here.

After a shocked breath, his lips began to move against mine. Strong arms encircled my waist, pulling me close. Pressed against his body, I no longer felt like myself. Like somehow I wasn't my own person but instead a welcomed part of him. Or maybe it was the other way around. Perhaps he was becoming a part of me.

Pulling back, he inhaled sharply. "Wait. We can't do this. It's not allowed."

"Says who?" my dream self boldly asked.

The shadow around us shimmered, his now-dark eyes flaring silver. Then suddenly he was gone, leaving me alone to question everything I knew—which clearly wasn't much.

The cold press of my lips against my mirror jerked me back to reality. The wood planks beneath my feet were frigid, the fire in the hearth reduced to barely an ember. I waited for something else miraculous to happen, another shift in my dream that would bring him back. Instead, I startled when my familiar rubbed himself between my ankles, winding in and out of my legs as cats normally do.

"Jenks, what are you doing in my dream?" I picked him up and nuzzled his black fur. "You're meant to stand guard over me, not join me."

I focused on the room again, the space coming into sharp relief as my eyes continued to adjust in the dark. Mr. Jenkins had never entered my dreams before, and as he writhed in my arms, I realized he hadn't still. This was not a dream. I was wide awake... and a complete fool.

[12]

2

THE WEAVER—TWO WORDS BOUND TO PLAGUE me for the rest of the day.

I considered drinking another cup of elixir but instinctively knew it would no longer work. He seemed to be in total control when it came to my dreams. Instead, I decided to set about my daily tasks. With the sun rising, a soft fog lingered between the trees, the dew on the ground still glistening and wet. The chirp of crickets provided an early morning soundtrack I happily busied myself to, working inside as I waited for the day to warm. Dusting my shelves and reorganizing my oils and herbs filled a good portion of my morning, though regardless of the mundane tasks, I couldn't stop thinking about him.

Had he really been here? In my home? Or was it all in my head—my perfect dream man brought to life? If not, I needed answers, like how had he broken through my wards? All I could do was hope he was true to his word… that we *would* see each other again tonight.

I looked to my altar and considered crafting another spell. A new one. One powerful enough to give me more control. Mr.

Jenkins meowed from beneath the kitchen table, and I knew he was right: None of my attempts would work against the Weaver. I needed to shift my focus to learning instead.

With the house dusted and cleaned, I dressed for the day in my favorite cornflower-blue dress, pulling my black lace-up boots into place beneath its well-worn hem. The ensemble was witchy enough to deter the people in our modern town from trying to engage with me, which was exactly how I preferred it. Though I'd lived here my entire life, I was still considered an outsider. A lesson I learned a long time ago.

Living quietly alone on the outskirts of Arcadia Forest, Mom and I had crafted a solitary life of magic and gardening that fulfilled any desire of connection either of us ever had. My dad died when I was three from a war injury even Mama's magic couldn't heal. But together, she and I learned to survive and grow until she passed away when I was thirteen.

Left to fend for myself, I drew on everything she taught me and continued my home education with regular visits to the local library in West Greenwich. One day—when I was feeling brave—I attempted to make friends but was starkly reminded of just how different I was. Not only did I have one blue and one green eye, but a young girl living alone in the woods caused people to talk... *harshly*. But thanks to my magic, no one entered our grounds uninvited.

My only friend in town remained the librarian, Keelyn. She had witnessed my awkward demise at the hands of the townies that day and ever since had been the only person I chose to talk to on a regular basis.

"Good morning, Milly. How's the bean crop coming along?" Keelyn smiled, the delicate lines at the corners of her eyes pulling tight as she waited for my response.

I snagged one of the carts from beside the front door. "It's good. Thank you. I'm getting ready to harvest some fresh peppers later today. I'll save you a bag if you'd like to stop by."

Vegetables, flowers, crystals, and creams were how I made a living. The small farmers market held in the area produced a weekly income that comfortably got me by.

"That sounds wonderful! I get off at four. Will that work?"

I thought about the timing. A few hours here for research, then home to harvest and sort... "Yes. That should be fine. I'll put on some tea."

Keelyn's eyes brightened as she gave me a wink then waved me on as another patron neared her desk. She'd been the librarian here since she was a teenager, and now in her early forties, she was well-respected within the community. I was happy to call her my friend.

Ducking into the far back corner of the old redbrick schoolhouse, I settled into my usual spot. The round table offered an unobstructed view of the second-story windows on either side of the belfry but concealed me enough from the ongoings on the main floor that I wouldn't be disturbed.

I placed my notebook and pen down beside my water bottle and wheeled the cart into the nearby stacks. Most of the books I read were located here, hidden in the shadows of the New Age section. Metaphysics, astrology, and anything regarding a "kitchen witch" had graced my reading list since a very young age. Thankfully, Keelyn never judged me for what some might find *odd* selections. Today's research, however, would be even more focused.

Running my fingers along the spines, I quickly found the dream section and pulled a few new titles from the shelves. I'd studied lucid dreaming and dream symbology, as well as how to unlock the power of your dreams, but unfortunately, none of those books mentioned a Weaver. Honestly, I wasn't sure if I was on the right track at all, but somehow this felt like the correct place to start.

With my selections spread out on the table, I hovered my hands above them and closed my eyes. The magical signature of each book was different, and with my intention set, I focused on finding the one giving off the strongest vibe.

Ripples of energy met my palms, and when my skin warmed, I opened my eyes.

The book was the oldest among them, with worn edges and a tattered spine. I wasn't surprised. All true magic was documented so long ago that hardly any original texts still existed. However, with books like these—beautiful reproductions from a witch's point of view—we could still get close to true information, even in the modern world today.

This one in particular was written by Genevieve DuWant, a pseudonym for sure, but I found the title oddly subdued for the subject matter within. *Magic of the Mind* didn't exactly scream "dreamscapes" or "Weaver."

I flipped open the cover, reading the introduction:

> The mind is a wonderful thing as long as you don't lose control of it.

Hmm... What could any of what I'd experienced have to do with losing my mind? I was suddenly unsure if this book was going to be of any help at all, but I read on.

> Dreaming is a way for your mind to let go, taking you through a subconscious minefield planted by your memories and fears, your hopes and dreams. But never once were we told it could also be where you lose yourself or that it could be controlled by another.

Now we were getting somewhere.

> While I cannot prove what I say is true, I can document my experiences and share them here as a warning—a warning that mind magic does exist and can be woven in and out of your dreams by the one given ultimate control.

She hadn't mentioned the Weaver by title or name, only using the word *woven* instead. And while the *one given ultimate control* could be talking about the Weaver, it could also be a metaphor for gaining control over one's self. I skimmed through the rest of the book, but in the end, I decided if what she had written couldn't be proven, it wasn't going to do me any good. I placed the tome back on the shelf and moved on to the other books in my pile.

Three hours later, I still had no additional information on my Weaver.

My Weaver. A warmth flushed through me.

Was it odd that it really did feel that way? That some strange man within my dreams felt like he belonged to me? Or odder yet… that I somehow belonged to him?

Returning home, I buried my hands in the garden dirt, harvesting the peppers, beets, and beans I'd need to shell over the next few days. My mind drifted over the information—or lack thereof—I had read in the library today. Not a single book produced anything useful, but the words *mind magic* kept needling my brain. Could the Weaver be a real person using this type of magic to manipulate my dreams? If so, I had to find out why. Or more specifically… why me?

"Milly, are you back there?" Keelyn's voice pulled me from my thoughts.

"Hi, yes. Just beyond the fence."

Keelyn pushed through the wooden gate, joining me in the garden and bringing with her a welcome reprieve. I needed to focus on something else for a while before I went utterly mad. *The mind is a wonderful thing as long as you don't lose control of it.* I chuckled as the words from the old book drifted through my head again.

"What's so funny?" Keelyn pulled her long silver-blond hair into a ponytail, then bent down to relieve me of the burlap bag I was dumping the beans into.

"Just something I read today that stuck with me." I tossed another handful of the legumes into the sack.

"Well, I have to say it's good to see you laugh." Jiggling the bag to settle the contents, she cinched the top between her hands. "Can I help you inside with these?"

"Yes, thank you. I'll put on the tea." I led her inside, thinking about what she said. I supposed she was right—it had been a long time since I felt this joyful. Not that I was unhappy in my life, but as the wheel of the year turned and the seasons repeated, the days could edge toward doldrum. The Weaver's appearance had brought on something unexpected. Something new and wonderful to look forward to. Something to laugh at and bring a smile to my face.

"Did you not enjoy your books today? I noticed you didn't check out any of them." Keelyn dropped the bag of beans on the floor, steadying them against the kitchen cabinet with her leg.

"Oh… I was just doing a little research, but nothing panned out." I shrugged.

"Really? Is there a certain book you'd like me to order instead?"

Her offer was kind, but I had no idea if one even existed, so I kept my answer vague. "Sure, if you come across any dream-type books that mention the word *weaver*, that would be great."

Keelyn tilted her head. She had always accepted how different I was with my solitary ways and soft-spoken oddness, but I never shared my magic with her. With anyone, actually. And as much as I enjoyed her company, I still didn't feel comfortable doing so now.

"Here's your batch of peppers." I shoved a grocery bag of freshly picked sweet peppers into her hand, my oddness striking again.

"Thanks!" She laughed. "These will go great in my next salad. Speaking of—would you like to join me for dinner tonight? I'm hosting a book club at my house and think you'd have a really good time."

Gnawing the inside of my cheek, I tried to be brave, but people just weren't my thing. Besides, I needed to prepare if I was going to search out the Weaver again tonight. "Thank you, but I'll have to pass. Harvest season affords me no breaks. I'll be off to bed early again."

Keelyn dipped her head, a knowing smile pulling at her rose-colored lips. "Well, if you ever change your mind, or when you finally do get a break, you're always welcome. We'll be meeting every week on Thursday nights."

I smiled, my cheeks flushing as she graciously accepted yet another of my excuses. "Thank you for stopping by. I'll be sure to save you some fresh currants next time, if you're still interested."

"Absolutely. I love using them in my yogurt cakes." Keelyn winked and gave me a little wave goodbye. "See you soon, Milly, and I'll let you know if I come across a book you described."

I waved to Keelyn just as the kettle began to whistle. Realizing I'd ruined an afternoon of what could have been lighthearted camaraderie with my friend, I poured myself a cup of the lavender-mint tea and filled the bowl on the table full of beans. Shelling the pods was a relaxing, monotonous task I'd done over and over, year after year, and I had the calluses to prove it. Rough around the edges, I was all work and no play, and while I truly did prefer being alone, sitting here in this empty house, I was regretting my friend's rushed departure. I couldn't deny I was considering Keelyn's offer to join her book club, and there was certainly no doubt I couldn't wait to see *him* again. It was all so unlike me, and I wondered how the Weaver had broken through that facet of my life.

Once processed, I stored the shelled beans in the freezer, planning to use them in my ham hock soup when the weather turned cold. Grabbing my wicker basket, I traipsed back into the garden to gather the ingredients I'd need for my spell tonight. My goal wasn't for more control but instead to open my heart and mind and to see things more clearly. Perhaps if I could pierce the veil of the dreamscape, I could see what was truly going on.

Snipping nine heads off my peppermint and lemongrass plants, I returned to the kitchen and dropped them into the mortar. Adding a chunk of ginger, I began to grind.

Reveal the truth. Allow me to see. Magic being hidden from me. Open my heart, and my mind. Show me the truth, nine by nine.

I muddled the herbs into a fine powder, setting the kettle again to steep on the stove. After adding a pinch into my cup, I dripped in a dollop of honey and poured hot water over it all. Sweet steam rose into the air, spinning at the base, then continuing upward into a smoky, straight line. The spell was energetically clear.

Normally I'd work in the garden past nightfall, but tonight I was ready to start my next adventure by 7:00 p.m.—a good, magical number.

"Now you stay close tonight, okay?" I scratched Jenks behind the ears and tucked myself beneath the blankets as he walked atop them, settling near my feet. I quickly drifted off, the dream enveloping me like a blooming cloud—a watercolor painting rendered right before my eyes.

Rolling green hills and a bluish-gray sky surrounded me. I thought I might be stateside until I saw a unique stone castle perched atop the nearest hill. The air was balmy and carried with it the thick, cloying fragrance of my favorite flowers.

I turned and gasped.

An ocean of blush-pink roses spread up over a hill as far as the eye could see, some so plump they looked like peonies. I buried my nose in the nearest cluster, inhaling the familiar scent. "How did you know these were my favorite?" I asked, feeling the Weaver's presence behind me before even seeing him.

"I know a lot about you." His deep voice drifted to my ears.

That statement put me on edge, but as a clear sense of contentment settled over me, I knew my spell had worked. I was seeing the truth beneath his words and was confident I had nothing to fear.

Spinning slowly, I kept my eyes down but tried to catch a glimpse of him in my periphery. A flash caught my eye, and I looked up to find a gorgeous Victorian greenhouse standing nearby. Traipsing along the manicured path, I let my fingers graze the soft petals, making sure to avoid the hidden thorns. Entering the glass greenhouse, I inhaled deeply, enjoying more roses, foxglove, periwinkle, and poppies, all in full bloom and filling the space. The skirt of my sundress swished lightly against the leaves as I nonchalantly moved between the manicured rows. Hummingbirds flitted among a rose of Sharon while the largest monarch butterfly I'd ever seen slowly opened and closed its wings from its spot in a wild honeysuckle bush.

"I have so many questions." I began. "Exactly how do you know a lot about me? And what type of magic are you using to control my dreams?" I hoped my directness didn't scare him off, but I needed to understand.

Silence settled throughout the space, taking with it even the slightest rustle of leaves. Behind me, a wall of energy pressed against my back. Slowly, nervously, I turned around and came face to face with the Weaver.

He stood in front of an enormous rip in space, his eyes matching the stars behind him. A swirling galaxy of silver with the faintest hint of blue and purple shimmered against a black expanse. He lifted a muscled arm from beneath his cloak, extending his hand to me. "I have all the answers you seek. You only need to surrender and join me."

Surrender?

I wasn't sure I liked the sound of that.

3

I STOOD FROZEN, UNABLE TO MOVE. REGARDLESS of his rugged good looks, angled jawline, and the sexy, light scruff framing his chin and mouth, I wasn't about to willingly walk into the unknown. I knew the dreamscape could be a dangerous place.

Running his hand through his short dark hair, he lowered his arm back to his side. "I thought you wanted answers."

"I do. But oddly enough, I don't think they lie through there." I pointed to the swirling cosmos behind him, positive I was offending him in some way.

With his hood back, I could see the twitch in his jaw and the tightening of muscles beneath his broad shoulders as he contemplated what to do. Standing over six feet tall and in all black, he stared down at me with a slight grin pulling at his lips.

Lips I suddenly wanted to kiss.

I started toward him, leaning in, then caught sight of the stars shimmering behind him and stopped. "Wait. Are you doing this? Enchanting my dreams again?"

His smirk grew wider. "And what if I am?"

"Then I'd ask that you kindly stop and take me seriously. I want answers, and I will not be bamboozled by your tricks or charms."

"Bamboozled?"

"Yes, bamboozled!" I mentally stomped my foot. "I demand to know the truth."

The slice behind him wavered, changing from an expanse of stars to a deeply shadowed forest instead. "Then I suggest you swallow your fears and follow me." He spun on his heel, walked through the rip in space, and disappeared into the new scene waiting beyond.

I took a deep breath and closed my eyes, searching for the truth. My well of magic fluttered softly in my gut as I focused on the rip before me. No warnings flared, and I couldn't deny I was desperate for answers. Swallowing hard, I walked forward and followed him into the unknown.

Evergreens surrounded me, stretching into the sky, interspersed with white trunks and the vibrant yellow leaves of a beautiful aspen grove. "Where are we?"

"My home."

"You live in the woods alone… like me?"

"Alone. Yes. But my home here is sheltered. Hidden from the outside world."

I could feel it in my bones, the chill on my face, the animals scurrying through the woods—his home might be outside of our realm, but this place was real. I spun in a circle, trying to decipher exactly where I was, but I didn't have a clue.

"This is real." It came out as a statement, not a question, but he answered anyway.

"Correct."

I knew it. He *was* real. My cheeks reddened as I remembered the cold feel of the glass against my lips during our made-up kiss.

I pulled up the collar of the jacket I now wore, spinning to face him. "If this is real, then how are we still inside my dream?" I snapped the lapels of my coat to emphasize my seriousness. "Where does your magic come from?"

"Like yours, it's been handed down from generation to generation. But unlike you, only one can hold the magic and title of Weaver at a time."

"Why? If it flows from your family, why would only one be given the right?"

"Those are the rules, Milly. And having more than one Weaver has never been allowed. It's simply not possible."

I searched his sparkling eyes for the hint of a lie but, again, only saw truth in his words. "So *Weaver* is your title. And the magic is passed from generation to generation. That means you must have been selected, right?"

"Correct again."

"By whom?"

"The one who came before me."

I mulled over his words. "So it's a retirement thing. A position passed from one witch to another?" The trees swayed, bringing with them the sharp scent of pine and a cold wind that sent a shiver up my spine. Maybe I was pushing my luck.

Luckily, the Weaver chuckled. "Yes, I suppose you could think of it that way." His rich, deep tone brought with it a shiver all its own.

I pulled my coat tighter. "Is there somewhere else we could go?"

He looked to a thin footpath hidden beneath a shuffle of leaves, the muscles of his jaw twitching again. Perhaps I'd discovered his "deep thought" tell.

"Yes. But you must understand. The home you see here is only accessible from this plane. You will not be able to find me in the real world."

"Fine, as long as it's warm." I rubbed my hands together, frustrated I had no control over our current interaction and even more annoyed he hadn't bothered to give me gloves.

In the next instant, wool gloves appeared on my hands, and the Weaver stalked away through the woods, a king in his domain.

The temperature remained cold as we walked on, the crispness speaking of mountains and fresh air. With a dusky-blue sky as the backdrop against the trees, I thought it had to be late afternoon.

"If this *is* a real place, then where exactly are we?"

He stopped, spinning to face me. "Why does it matter? I already told you, you cannot find it in the real world," he stated flatly.

My gut told me he wouldn't answer, but I had to try.

"I was just wondering." I shrugged.

"Well, don't." He stared at me for a moment, his brows creased in worry and a fleck of sadness hinted in his eyes.

"Okay. Sorry. But remember *you* brought *me* here," I whispered.

He lowered his head. "I know. I'm sorry."

Picking back up, I followed him in silence as we wove deeper into the woods. Stepping over branches and leaves, I focused on the crunch beneath my boots until we emerged in a small clearing that seemed to serve as the Weaver's front yard. Beyond it sat the quaintest, most adorable cabin I'd ever seen. The small A-frame with its dark roof, black siding, and warm honeyed trim framing the eaves and sills stood proud and alone, boldly carving out its tiny spot among the massive trees.

"Welcome to my cabin." The Weaver shuffled on his feet like a nervous child.

"It's lovely."

He gestured for me to enter, but as I neared the front door, I caught sight of movement from the corner of my eye. Looking up, I gasped. The entire back side of the house was surrounded by an expanse of dark, shimmering water. "You live on a lake?"

His jaw ticked. "You could say that."

Lured by the water, I entered the cabin and walked straight to the wall of windows at the rear of the house. The Weaver slid open the large glass door, stepping out onto the rustic back porch. Joining him, I stared across the lake and up into the sky, wrapping my arms around my middle. Snow-tipped mountains stood in the distance, surrounding us on all sides. "This is the most beautiful place I've ever seen."

The Weaver stood silent as I gazed upon the serene landscape. Fireflies lit the night sky, mocking the stars forever out of their reach. The calmness here was unmatched and unlike anything I'd ever experienced before. Even at home in my garden, I never felt a peace like this.

"I'm glad you like it. It's the only place we can spend time together, but we can come back as often as you'd like."

I cocked my head. "What do you mean?"

He moved to join me at the edge of the porch, gripping the modern metal railing with strong tan hands. "It's forbidden for me to spend time with anyone in the real world. Only in the dreamscape can I interact with my queen."

"I'm sorry... what?"

"My magic comes with rules, Milly. One of them being that I can't interact in the real world. But here, in the dreamscape, we can be together." He smiled down at me nonchalantly, completely skipping the *queen* part of his previous statement.

"What did you mean... interact with your *queen?*"

"Each Weaver has to have a counterpart to achieve his full potential. And I choose you."

With wide eyes, I turned back to the lake, dumbfounded.

How on earth had this man chosen me to be his anything? He didn't even know me. Besides my magic, there was nothing special about me, and I certainly didn't rank as anyone's queen.

"Why me?" I whispered, hoping my truth spell was still in effect.

"Because you're the only one who passed the tests."

I lowered my head, the crushing blow of his words hitting like a rock and sinking in my gut. I chastised my romantic self for secretly wishing for some sort of *soul connection* or a *from the first time I saw you, I knew* statement... but tests?

"What kind of tests?" I asked, fortifying my tender heart.

"It takes someone with strong magic to see me in their dreams—which you have done numerous times." He moved closer, lifting my chin with the curve of his finger. "You wanted the truth, Milly, and that's about as much as I have."

I met his sparkling eyes, struggling to slow my racing heart. "Or at least as much as you're willing to share, right?"

"I want to share everything with you." He gestured to the dark expanse beyond the deck, then turned and walked back inside.

Of course, I followed.

"If this is the only place we can interact, are there limits to what we can do here? Inside the dreamscape too?" I hated how small my voice had become, but I had to know.

A cocky leer stretched across his beautiful face. "No. There are no limits here." He settled into a buttery leather couch and flicked his hand at the stone hearth that climbed from floor to ceiling. Flames sparked to life, filling the space with a warm glow. "The entire dreamscape is my domain, so where would you like to go?"

Go? I thought back to ancient Greece and the English countryside full of flowers. "We can travel anywhere?"

"Anywhere you'd like." His smile grew as he flicked an invisible piece of lint off his black cloak before it disappeared completely, leaving him in black pants and a black button-down shirt. His rolled sleeves revealed muscular tan forearms, which my eyes greedily scanned. For a moment, I thought I glimpsed a tattoo there, but a second later, it was gone, leaving only his smooth golden skin.

I walked to a papasan chair near the fireplace and sank into its cream-colored cushion. "Actually, do you mind if we just stay here and talk?" I had so many questions and wanted to learn as much as I could while given the chance.

"If that's what you'd like to do." The timbre of his voice changed, his smile turning slightly seductive.

Suddenly, I wasn't sure if I was ready to be alone with him or not. For all my longing and curiosity, I'd never been with a man before. At least not a man like him. My first real-life crush involved a toss in the hay with Peter O'Toole, but it was nothing significant. Hurried, awkward, and solely for the purpose of getting past our teenage "firsts," he was the only boy in town who ever paid any attention to me and the only one who didn't live between the pages of a book.

I shifted in my seat, uncomfortable with the look the Weaver was giving me. *Goddess, I hope he can't read my mind.* "Actually. I think I'd like to go back to that English garden, if that's okay," I sputtered quickly.

[32]

He chuckled beneath his breath, then dipped his head and pushed to stand. "Your wish is my command." Rising from the couch, he extended his hand. "But we'll have to walk back to the clearing first."

"Why?"

His throat bobbed. "Rules, Milly. I can't pierce the dreamscape from inside my home." He dropped his offered hand and walked out the front door, the fire dying behind us.

"I see." I didn't really but felt it was something I shouldn't push. I followed him out in silence, the front door clicking shut behind us of its own accord.

"Why the English garden?" he asked over his shoulder.

I shrugged. "Plants and flowers are my life. It's how I make a living in the real world." I kicked a pinecone from my path. "They remind me of my mother."

The Weaver took a deep, audible breath. "I'm sorry for your loss."

I didn't question how he knew she was gone. If he'd been watching me for any length of time at all, he already knew.

"Thank you. But it was a long time ago."

"That doesn't make it any easier. In fact, I'm impressed you thrived so well all on your own."

I stopped walking, curious as to what he meant. "Why shouldn't I have been able to *thrive* on my own?"

The Weaver turned, surprise etched on his face. "I'm sorry. I didn't mean to offend you."

His cloak reappeared, and he quickly yanked up the hood, all but his eyes disappearing beneath it. I was beginning to think this might be more of a security blanket instead of a piece of his Weaver attire, as I'd originally assumed.

"I've witnessed a lot of young people lose their families, Milly, but I don't believe any of them remained as strong as you."

Something warm rose in my chest. I couldn't tell if it was anger, sadness, or pride—possibly a mixture of all three. "Yes, well, my mother taught me well."

"Yes. It seems she did."

Silence descended as we continued to the clearing, the temperature dropping another few bone-chilling degrees as the last of the sun's rays faded behind the trees.

"Here we are." With a swipe of his hand, the Weaver ripped open another slice in space, the English countryside visible beyond. "Ladies first."

This time I felt no fear as I stepped through, grateful to be somewhere warm and familiar in the oddest way. Odd because it was clear I was still dreaming, yet this place felt familiar, still filled with my favorite things.

I ran a hand across the velvet petals of a plump English rose, inhaling its sweet scent. "Thank you for bringing me back here. Out of all the dreams you've created for me, I think this one is my favorite."

The Weaver didn't answer right away, his soft footsteps shuffling a few paces behind me.

"I'm glad you like it. But I don't create the dreams, Milly. I simply weave the magic required to pull them from your soul."

4

I SPUN AROUND, STRUGGLING FOR WORDS. "UM… isn't that… *dangerous?* To mess with a person's soul?" The idea of the Weaver holding sway over my soul, even in the smallest of ways, frightened me to my core, but I wanted to understand. I *needed* to understand.

"I don't *mess* with your soul, Milly. I just use my magic to access your deepest desires and bring them to life within your dreams."

I stopped moving and put my hands on my hips. "So you think my deepest desire is to be waited on by tanned pool boys in ancient Greece or fawned over by some long-lost desert prince?"

The Weaver strode forward, coming to stand directly in my path. A heaviness filled the space, his silver eyes swirling as they met mine.

I held my breath.

"Deep down, I think you are lonely, and my magic has a way of turning that into companionship within your dreams. Whether it be a forest full of playful fairy-tale creatures or a handsome prince, your soul is crying out for a partner, Milly. And I hope you pick me."

I stood silent, gawking at the beautiful man in front of me as he crossed his arms over his broad chest. He wanted to be my partner. My counterpart, my *king*. And I think I wanted that too. Whether through my spell or not, there was something genuine about him. Something innocent despite his attempted bravado so far.

A gentle smile pulled at my lips. "As desperate as it makes me sound, I'm glad I passed your *tests* and you finally revealed yourself to me. I was starting to think I was going crazy... seeing the same man in every single one of my dreams." I turned back to the next row of flowers, hiding my reddening cheeks.

"I'm glad too, Milly. Truly. I feel like I've been looking for you my entire life. And now... we can start your training."

I spun back to face him. "Training?"

"Yes." His eyes danced. "As my partner, you'll need to learn how to hone your magic to use it in the dreamscape, balancing mine."

"I can use real magic here?" The words stumbled out of me, the idea strange on my tongue. Every time I attempted it before, it sputtered out, reminding me I was inside a dream.

The Weaver reached for my hand. "As my partner, yes. You'll be able to do anything you want. Even now, since we've found each other, your magic should react differently here."

Warmth radiated from our joined hands, spreading up my arm and into my chest, causing my breasts to heave.

I gazed up at him from beneath my lashes. "I think I would like that very much."

"Great. We'll start tomorrow."

"Why not now?" I asked, eager to stay with him for as long as I could and to learn something new.

"It's late. You need to rest, and I need to prepare."

My brows dipped, my excitement waning. "What do you mean? Is it going to hurt?"

"No, no. Nothing like that. It's just… I simply need to make sure there are no complications."

I pulled my hand from his, rubbing the same spot in my chest that had now turned hollow and cold.

"Trust me, Milly. We're going to be great together."

Trust him. Did I? I wanted to, but I wasn't sure quite yet. He seemed to be right about one thing, though: My soul did long for companionship. And wasn't the intention of my spell tonight to reveal the truth? *Yes, it was,* I reminded myself, and I *did* want this. Admitting that was the first step toward trust—trusting myself and trusting him to see where this could go. Now I just had to take the leap.

"Okay. But if I need my rest, does that mean I'll wake from this dream or simply fall into a deeper sleep?" Obviously, I had so much to learn.

"For now, you'll slumber peacefully, waking as usual once your day begins." My head bobbed in understanding, and a warm smile spread across his face. "Good night, Milly. I'll see you tomorrow."

I lifted a hand and waved goodbye, happy to know I'd see him again soon.

The Weaver was right. I spent the rest of the night in a deep, dreamless sleep, waking at the crack of dawn, excited for my day.

"Hello, Jenks." I ran a hand down my familiar's back, his black fur soft and warm beneath my touch. "You did a good job last night, keeping me safe." He nuzzled my side as I scratched behind his ears. "I have so much to tell you."

Pushing from the bed, I walked to the kitchen and set the kettle to boil. I had no idea how I was going to occupy my mind all day, but at least I could keep my hands busy harvesting my basil, oregano, parsley, and the last of the thyme left on the stalks. After showering, dressing, and enjoying my morning cup of tea, I pulled on my mukluks and grabbed my basket sitting next to the back door.

"Come on, Jenks. You can help me finish the herbs while I tell you everything that happened."

Jenks wound himself between my legs as I reached for the knob and opened the door.

We both froze.

A wall of white mist greeted me, the temperature dropping by at least fifteen degrees. I could barely spy the spindly trees lining the edge of my garden while a dense fog settled over the rest of the land like cotton candy filling a bowl. "Well, shoot. Looks like we won't be harvesting today after all."

Jenks and I slunk back inside, both saddened by the time we'd be missing in the garden.

Dropping the basket and shucking my boots, I quickly stoked the fire instead. "How about some breakfast, sweet boy?"

Jenks meowed his approval of my newly formed plan.

I dropped strips of bacon into the cast-iron skillet, the sizzle and aroma instantly brightening my mood. "So are you ready to hear about my latest adventure?"

Meow.

"Okay… so it started out in the English countryside. There were flowers everywhere and the most gorgeous glass greenhouse I'd ever seen—" The bacon snapped, a pop of grease making me jump. "Then the Weaver created a rip in space and took me to his private cabin in the woods…" I continued to regale Jenks with my adventure as I cooked, and by the time breakfast was over, I'd shared everything that had happened.

"I'll admit I'm a little nervous to start whatever this *training* is supposed to be." I ran a hand down Jenks's fur, readjusting myself on the couch. "But as always, I'll feel better knowing you're my anchor here."

Jenks bumped my palm with his head, then jumped down and padded to my altar. Clearly, he thought we had some magic to do.

With the strike of a match, I lit the end of my smudge stick, its musky scent filling the room.

In the name of the God and Goddess, please remove any negative energy from my body and space so that we may be filled with only love and light. So mote it be.

Jenks meowed, sealing the spell and my ring of protection.

Placing a piece of hematite on my altar, I lit the green candle next to it and whispered my request.

Lord and Lady, please aid me in grounding and centering my spirit. Keep me attached to my familiar so I may always find my way home.

Mama's voice drifted to my ears. *"Always speak your magic aloud, Milly, for there is power in your words."* I smiled at the memory.

Staring into the flame, I watched it dance as if it were a living creature. Letting my body waver and move, I focused on my feet touching the ground. The floor was solid beneath me, and in it, I found a grounding strength.

Lying down on the threadbare rug, I let each part of my body press against the firm wood planks. Closing my eyes, I imagined roots growing from each point, extending down into the earth. With every breath, I felt my connection grow. To my home, the earth, and the universe beyond.

Fear and anxiety drained away, filtered by the power of the earth as I focused on my breathing. Negative energy out, positive energy in. A golden thread connected to my core, pulsing with magic and completing the cycle.

"Being grounded isn't just about feeling calm but rather strengthening our connection to all things." Mother's wise words again floated to mind. *"To*

be grounded is to feel woven into the very fabric of the cosmos, Milly. There you will find peace and grace."

Letting myself drift, I fell further into the meditative spell—floating between two worlds just like when I was with the Weaver.

Golden sparks burst behind my lids, illuminating a sky in a massive swath of swirling purple and blue.

"I didn't expect to see you until tonight." The Weaver's voice sounded in my ear, but I kept my eyes shut tight. I knew he wasn't here but was somehow connecting with me through this dreamlike state.

"You *will* see me tonight, but for now, how about you give a girl a little alone time to meditate in peace?"

A sexy chuckle echoed in my head, followed by, "Enjoy your girl time, Milly. I'll be waiting."

A warm sensation filled me from head to toe, and while I could blame it on my grounding spell, I knew it was because of him.

Mr. Jenkins purred, pulling me back to reality, and when I opened my eyes, I found his little whiskers twitching inches from my face.

"What?"

His obstinate yowl made it clear he didn't like the Weaver interrupting our spell.

"I'm sorry. I didn't know he'd have access to me there." I sat up and ran a hand down my familiar's back. "Besides, the whole purpose of this spell was to strengthen our connection so you can keep me grounded when I'm with him. *And... you just proved you could.*"

Jenks wound his way around me, purring and nudging me with his little head.

"Yes, sweet boy. I'm so proud of you. You did such a good job."

Releasing the last tendrils of my spell, I noticed the time—it was barely after noon. If I spent the rest of the day completing my normal chores, it would be close to bedtime once I restocked all my wares for this weekend's farmers market. There were only a few left this season, so I needed to make them count.

Occupying myself, I dusted, swept, and washed every single dish I owned. Then I stacked the baskets and linens next to the front door before heading into the back room to determine what was ready to sell.

I opened the burlap bags, checking the green beans first. They looked good. The arugula and cabbage were also ready to go, but there weren't enough leeks left to make the trip. Still, with the vegetables I had and my usual creams and crystals, I'd earn my weekly income easily enough, which made it all worthwhile.

"Milly, one cannot survive on magic alone. You need to earn your place in this world if you are to ever fit in with the community around you. One wrong move and the questions elicited could lead to a full-on witch hunt."

Mama's words always needled my mind whenever I was tempted to take a shortcut in life. I learned at a young age money wasn't a true requirement when you had magic, but it was something you had to earn for yourself. Otherwise, the price for that magic may be far more than you were willing to pay.

Packing and hauling vegetables to the front door filled the rest of my day, and by early evening, I'd completed the creams I wanted to take this weekend as well. Lavender and shea for a relaxing face cream, cayenne-infused body butter for aches and pains, and, one of my favorites, peppermint and eucalyptus for headaches and colds. Not that I got sick often, but I loved the scent and wondered if my preemptive use of it helped in that fact.

The crystals I'd accumulated over the last month would make a good addition to my offerings as well. And as I laid them out across the table on my black cloth, one in particular caught my eye.

A smooth piece of bloodstone pulsed with energy. No surprise, I supposed, seeing as bloodstone was one of the most-used crystals in dream magic. But still, it had me wondering what revelations or new perceptions I was supposed to take note of on my adventure tonight.

I tucked the stone in my pocket, finished my prep work, and moved on to dinner. Soup and grilled cheese was an easy favorite, and after one final cleanup of the kitchen, I was ready for bed.

"All right, Jenks, here we go. Stay close, okay?"

Mr. Jenkins meowed and nestled into my side, nudging my open palm where the bloodstone now lay. Closing my eyes, it didn't take long for me to drift off and enter the dreamscape. The Weaver greeting me back in the English garden the minute I did.

[44]

"Good evening, my lady. Did you enjoy the rest of your day?" His honeyed tone and term of endearment warmed me against the slight chill in the air.

I looked down at the vintage dressing gown—one you might see Marie Antoinette wearing while she tended her cottage garden— and quickly pulled the accompanying coat around my middle, tying it at the waist. "Who is responsible for my clothing here?" I asked. "Are you doing this, or is it coming from me?"

The Weaver smiled. "A little of both."

"Well, perhaps that's where we can begin my training. Teach me how to change out of this." I shivered.

"But why? It's so becoming," he teased, his eyes sparkling from beneath his hood.

"Yes, well, you're not the one dealing with a draft."

A rumble of laughter enveloped me, warming me further from the inside out. "Fine. Simply close your eyes and let your magic rise to the surface. Once there, I'll combine it with mine."

I hesitated. "Will I need to say a spell?"

"No, Milly. Once we're linked, your magic only requires a thought."

Linked? Combined? Again, my nerves rose to the surface, not liking the sound of that.

5

"WHAT EXACTLY DO YOU MEAN BY LINKED?"

The Weaver stepped forward, taking my hand. My own magic began to rise as swirls of cosmic dust surrounded our entwined fingers, weaving in and out and around our wrists.

"As I've said, sharing your magic with me is what will bring balance to mine." He smiled. "It's all good things. And as partners, we can weave entire new worlds together."

The magic trailed between our hands, shifting from a silver flow to a deep purple and blue. The cosmic dust swelled, expanding farther into a whole new galaxy. Tiny planets swirled within the miniature world, shooting stars blazing trails between our fingertips. I stared into the cloud, shocked beyond words.

"There is no limit to our combined power, Milly. You just need to trust me in order for it to work."

Trust. There was that word again.

I pulled my hand away, the stars fading back to nothing more than a speck. "I mean no disrespect, but why *should* I trust you? Honestly, we barely know each other. And right now, I don't even trust myself. This is all so new. So rushed. And while I do want to be here, I still don't know enough about your world for this to all make sense yet." I reached for his hand again. "I'm flattered you want me to be your queen, but I'm just not sure about anything right now."

Roarke's head dipped, his faced painted in genuine sorrow.

It wasn't my intent to hurt him, but if we were talking truths, I had to be willing to speak my own. And it wasn't as though my questions were only for him. I was questioning myself too. Why was I so willing to jump at this opportunity? Was it because I'd grown up isolated and alone, or was it something deeper? Something my heart understood before my head could catch up?

Pushing past my fears, I closed my eyes and searched for the point at which our magic connected. There, in the center of my palm, I felt a twitch. Right where the bloodstone lay back in the real world. I focused harder, reaching for the link. The twitch morphed into an intense throb, growing to an almost painful measure before subsiding abruptly.

My eyes shot open, and the magic was gone. "What was that?"

"I'm not sure. Do you have something on you that could be blocking our connection?"

His question brought me up short. "I fell asleep with a piece of bloodstone in my hand. It usually helps me in all my dream work, but I'm thinking *this*"—I gestured between us—"may be completely different, beyond that somehow. Because of you."

He hesitated a moment. "Yes. Most dream-type talismans won't have the same effect when you're in my presence. I'm sorry. I should have told you before."

I pulled my hand from his. "Perhaps you should just guide me around a bit. Show me what your magic can do before we try to connect again."

The urge to buy myself some time overwhelmed me. I needed to test things out before giving myself—and my magic—completely over to him.

"Okay. Where would you like to begin?"

I looked around the English countryside, not sure what he meant. "I don't know."

He stood still, his jaw twitching a moment before he took my hand again. "How about this?" With nothing more than a flick of his wrist, another slice appeared. And beyond it, my cottage.

"Wait, you're taking me back already?"

"No, I thought we could venture somewhere familiar first. Somewhere you'll be more comfortable exploring."

I glanced at the plush pink flowers surrounding me, their swollen petals wavering in the wind. "I'm comfortable right here."

The Weaver smiled and sealed the rip. "All right, Milly. Then let's go visit the queen."

Shadows enveloped me and wind whipped my face as we appeared atop the steps of the stone castle moments later.

"How did you do that?" I asked.

"Here, all you have to do is give thought to what you want, and it will be done." He pushed open a large wooden door and guided me inside.

The enormous castle was understated but somehow still lavish with its brass sconces and crystal chandeliers lighting wide carpeted hallways.

I stood still, taking it all in. "Whose castle is this?"

"This is Windsor Castle."

I gasped, recognizing the name. And, of course, I was immediately aware of the occupants within. "Okay, never mind. I don't want to be here. This is too much."

"Milly, being a dream weaver means I have access to every person on earth. And becoming my partner means you will too. It's something you're going to have to get used to." He shrugged. "Besides, it's not like we have to hang out and watch the queen sleep. I just thought perhaps you'd like to take a stroll through the garden on the east terrace. Or if you'd rather see the moat garden around the round tower, we could do that instead."

Again dumbfounded, I stood still as a statue, trying to process everything at once.

"What's wrong?" he asked.

I shook my head, my frustration bleeding through. "I'm sorry. I just don't understand. I thought this was *my* dream, but you're saying we're both somehow inside the queen's dream instead? How is that possible?"

The Weaver sighed, then, without warning, pulled me through another sliver in space. We emerged back in his hidden forest, and without a word, he stomped through the woods and headed straight for his cabin. Yanking the front door open, he walked inside, leaving it cracked as the only sign I should follow.

Treading lightly, I eased through, clicking it shut behind me. "I'm sorry if I've upset you. I'm simply trying to understand." I leaned back against the door, folding my hands in front of me.

A fire flared to life in the hearth as he flopped down onto the leather couch. "I'm not upset, Milly. I'm just trying to figure out the best way to explain all this to you. Without connecting our magic, it's… *difficult* for me to explain what I do. Difficult for you to understand what *we* can do."

I moved to sit beside him, reaching for his hand. "It's okay. How about we call it a night and try again tomorrow?" *Maybe things will work better if I'm not tethered to my familiar through my grounding spell,* I thought to myself.

"Actually, that's probably a good idea. And, Milly… you can call me Roarke."

Roarke.

His name lingered in my mind as I woke back in bed with Mr.

Jenkins purring at my side. The abrupt end to my dream reminded me of the last time I was yanked awake without warning, and I knew now that I had been right. The Weaver *had* kicked me out of my own dream before. At least this time I was expecting it, asked for it even. I needed time to recenter and prepare myself for our next encounter. Especially if I *did* decide to join my magic with his.

A shiver rolled through me.

Just thinking about it scared me. But as I reached for the grounding connection still in place, I knew it would be okay. Roarke wouldn't let anything bad happen to me. At least I didn't think so. As secure and confident as I was in my own magic, this was something far beyond anything I'd ever experienced, and I couldn't deny that put me on edge.

I snuggled back under the covers, clearing my mind, and cast a sleeping spell to help me relax.

"Calm my mind and bring me sleep. Allow me to drift, but only so deep. Grounded and safe, in my bed I lay. Rested I'll wake to a brand-new day."

I closed my eyes, praying our connection was real. But only time would tell.

6

"GOOD EVENING, MILLY. YOU MIGHT WANT TO summon a coat. You look a little chilled."

I opened my eyes and thankfully found myself dressed, but only in a light cotton sheath. I looked around, expecting to be back in the English garden, but was surrounded by tall cliffs reaching high into the night sky as an ocean churned at our feet.

"Where are we?"

A light-gray duster appeared in my hand as the Weaver replied, "Last night you seemed concerned about running into people in the dreamscape, so I thought tonight we would start here instead, away from prying eyes."

The dark expanse above me sparkled in an array of colors. From blue to purple, magenta to silver, all shining brightly as far as the eye could see. This strange, almost alien constellation was mysterious and mesmerizing. And for the first time since learning I was the Weaver's choice, I was truly excited to see what we could do.

"I'm ready to learn more."

Roarke smiled and took my hand. "These first few trips are just to show you how the dreamscape works. After that, we can try combining our magic again, if you're up for it."

I nodded, not knowing what to expect, but I meant what I said. I *did* want to learn more.

Roarke lifted our joined hands, and I felt a slight surge, then stood there gawking as he waved his other across the sky. The constellation shifted and changed, creating a whole new scene directly above us. Three pyramids dotted the desert before me, and Orion's belt aligned above them, shimmering wildly in the distance.

"What's this?" I asked.

"Just one of the billions of dreams being created tonight."

"Whose dream is it?"

"I'm not sure. That's not usually how it works."

I pulled my hand from his, frustrated again. "Then, as usual, I don't understand. What *exactly* is it that you do?"

Roarke lowered his muscular frame to the ground, the wet sand beneath him squelching under his weight. "That's what I've been trying to say, Milly. It's too hard to explain because it's not something I *do*. It's just something I *am*." His eyes lifted to the stars. "The magic of the Weaver simply *is*. In the dreamscape, my magic reacts automatically to all the souls in the world, creating dreams pulled from their subconscious. There's nothing I have to do or any spell I have to say. The magic simply flows from me because of who I am."

I stared into the Egyptian desert, its heat causing the edges of the scene to waver in the sky. "Then why do you need me?"

"Every Weaver has to have a partner to balance out their magic. If not, it creates an imbalance that can be felt in the real world. And I shouldn't have to tell you that any imbalance in nature is not a good thing."

He was right. Mama always talked about balance and harmony and how important it was to our existence in the world. The yin and yang of things. To work within the shadows *and* the light. And to always embrace the good along with the bad.

The question was now which one was all this.

"As the dreams form, I'm able to walk among them, shifting from one to another with only a thought. That's what I've been trying to show you." Roarke waved his hand again, and the pyramids disappeared. A dense, shadowy jungle replaced the scene, filled with squawks of exotic birds, the roar of an unknown jungle cat, and the trill of a multitude of bugs, all bringing it to life.

I hesitated for only a moment, my blood pumping heavily through my veins. "Can we go in there?" The excitement of visiting such a lush place yanked at my very soul.

Living alone for the past six years had been peaceful. Sedate. But the thought of visiting such a foreign place almost had me ready to combine my magic with Roarke's right there on the spot… *almost.* Sure, I could visit the Amazon rainforest in real life, but what made this so special was the extraordinary things you could only experience in a dream. Florescent-green trees wafting in the warm breeze. Vibrant blue bugs floating through the sky, lighting the scene with their neon colors even though it was the middle of the day. It was the fantasy of it all that made me brave.

"Of course." Roarke stood and spread his hands wider.

The scene above us grew in size—like a picture expanding on a screen—enveloping us into the iridescent dream. The colors were so vibrant they almost hurt my eyes. Parrots, macaws, and even the occasional hoatzin flew overhead, their usual impressive hues heightened to the point of glowing. Trails of blue, pink, and green floated behind them as they winged through the trees—like living comets painting the air with their neon cosmic dust.

"This is beyond beautiful." I gaped.

Roarke nudged my shoulder, glancing down at our hands. "May I?"

I smiled and nodded, a flush running through me when he intertwined his fingers with mine.

Walking hand in hand, Roarke led me deeper into the jungle, my stomach fluttering as wildly as the indigo butterflies landing in the trees. We walked in silence, letting the symphony of the jungle fill the air between us, until suddenly a wild roar sounded up ahead.

We followed the cat's call and found a pure-white jaguar lounging in a tree next to the most beautiful waterfall I'd ever seen. Turquoise water glinted and churned at its base, creating a pool at least three hundred feet below its crest.

"Come on." Roarke led me into the water, its balmy temperature adding to the magic.

"Don't we need to worry about him?" I pointed back to the jaguar, noticing my clothes had shifted to a one-piece bathing suit covered in large green leaves.

Roarke pulled me close, bringing us almost nose to nose. "Milly, when you're with me, you don't need to worry about a thing." His eyes sparked, and the sexy timbre of his voice had me dipping my head, peering into the water as I tried to hide my blushing cheeks.

Trails of silver glided over the water whenever we moved. I waded in farther, realizing there were no fish or other dangers to be seen. Diving beneath the surface, I relished in the freedom and wonder Roarke's magic had to offer. Emerging behind the waterfall, I leaned back against the stone cliff.

Lush ferns, vines of ivy, and twisting branches lined either side, allowing flowers to spread their beauty all the way down to the water's edge. I swam to the nearest bloom and buried my nose in its glossy petals. "These are amazing," I declared when Roarke's head broke the surface a few feet away.

"I'm glad you like them, but there are more wonders to be seen whenever you're ready."

I leaned back, allowing myself to float atop the water. The sheer beauty of this place and its utter peacefulness made me never want to leave. "Can't we stay a bit longer?" I asked, my eyes glued to his.

Roarke's jaw twitched, meaning he was giving his answer some serious thought. "We could, but there's so much I want to show you."

Righting myself, I doggy-paddled in front of him, wondering what those other things could be. "Do you mean there's more to see here, or are we going somewhere else?"

Roarke smiled and swam closer. "Milly, we can go wherever you want. You only have to think of a place."

"Okay. Um…" I stammered. With the world—the universe really—at our disposal, all the choices became overwhelming. "I don't really know. Maybe we could go back to the pyramids you showed me before?"

With a sexy grin pulling at his lips, the Weaver waved his hand again, instantly depositing us right in front of the sphinx.

I looked down, my clothing already adjusted to suit the climate, and stared back up in awe. The ancient half man-half lion was larger in person than I ever imagined. With the pyramids looming in the distance, the scene was so surreal. "I can't believe I'm actually here. I've wanted to visit for so long. Maybe raid some tombs, discover an ancient pharaoh, or better yet… find the hidden spell book of a long-dead priest." My nerves buzzed, excitement firing along every vein.

"That sounds like quite the adventure. Where do you want to start?" Roarke reached for my hand again, and the buzzing increased.

I looked out across the desert, half expecting a flashing arrow to point the way. But only the dry land of the ancient world lay before us, heaving as if it were breathing and waiting to see what we would do.

I summoned my courage, then, following my instincts, pulled Roarke forward and ran between the paws of the sphinx. A large inscribed granite slab stood at its base, solid against its chest. It was at least twelve feet tall and seven feet wide, covered in pictures and hieroglyphs.

"Do you know what it says?" I asked.

Roarke smiled and flicked his hand toward the stone, transforming the inscription into English for me to read.

> *"Year I, third month of the first season, day 19, under the Majesty of Horus, the Mighty Bull, begetting radiance, (the Favourite) of the Two Goddesses, enduring in Kingship like Atum, the Golden Horus, Mighty of Sword, repelling the Nine Bows; the King of Upper and Lower Egypt, Men-kheperu-Ra, the Son of Ra, Thothmes IV, Shining in Diadems; beloved of (Amon), given life, stability and dominion, like Ra, forever…"*

I looked up and down the rest of the twelve-foot tablet. "Wow. This is a lot."

Roarke laughed. "It definitely is. But I'll make it easy. A young prince fell asleep at the base of the sphinx's head and had a vision in which the sphinx promised to make him the ruler of Egypt if he cleared the sand from the rest of its body. He did so, and the rest is history. This epigraphic stele has stood between the paws of the sphinx ever since, telling his story. It was erected in 1401 BC and is called the Dream Stele."

The Dream *Stele?* I looked back at the granite slab, enamored now for a completely different reason. I wondered if the Weaver and his magic had anything to do with the prince's vision.

Roarke chuckled. "I know what you're thinking, but this was way before my time."

I cocked my hip, crossing my arms over my chest. "But admit it… With your magic, you have the ability to affect people's dreams. You're not just watching, are you?"

Roarke dipped his head, his smile shifting like the sands beneath our feet. "Yes. Weavers do have the *ability* to affect people's dreams. Perhaps to show them something they needed to see or help guide them toward a decision they're struggling to make." His eyes held mine. "But that doesn't mean that *I* do that. As you know, there are rules to a Weaver's magic, most automatically imposed by the title we carry, but some are placed by the individual themselves. And that is one of mine. I do *not* use my magic to alter people's dreams."

I stood still, staring at the stele, and prayed he was telling the truth.

7

A WARM WIND STIRRED AROUND US, BLOWING sand across my cheeks. It rubbed my skin like sandpaper, and I couldn't help but wonder if Roarke was behind the distraction. He always seemed to know what I was thinking.

"Are you ready to continue your adventure?" he asked tentatively.

I didn't answer because I honestly wasn't sure. Trepidation and doubt continued to creep into my mind between bouts of excitement and bravery. At some point, I would have to pick a side within myself.

Following my intuition again, I walked forward, peering past the edge of the large quartz stele, and found a small gap behind it. Gripping the edge, I pulled. Warm air blasted from a hidden entrance that had been shielded by the stele this entire time.

"Did you know this was here?"

Roarke smiled but kept silent.

I squeezed through the opening and into the secret corridor beyond. I couldn't remember anyone in the real world having discovered a passageway beneath the sphinx and wondered if it was just a part of the dream we were now in.

Swallowing past the lump in my throat, I turned back to Roarke and stretched out my hand. "Well? Are you coming?" I grinned.

Pure, unadulterated joy shone on his face as he threaded his fingers through mine and followed me inside. The thrill of a once-in-a-lifetime adventure won out over my fears, sparking something inside me that had only now begun to burn bright.

We ran through ancient tunnels, into secret crypts, and finally found a throne room buried deep beneath the earth. Treasures of unimaginable wealth filled every corner and crevice, including an entire desk of worn leather tomes.

Cracking the spine of the thickest one, I smiled as I stared at symbols and words from one of the oldest cultures in history. Roarke waved his hand again, transforming them for me to read.

Blood from blood, time to time,
Blessed is our lord Ra, the mighty divine.
Share his power, brought to thee,
From priests of Satu, three by three.

A picture of six priests standing over a pharaoh with their arms raised above their heads lined the bottom half of the page. I could only assume it was Satu they were casting the spell for.

This was such a treasure. I felt like Evelyn from *The Mummy*. The adventure, the romance, even the danger called to me. And now I was living it, if only in a dream.

I looked over my shoulder. "Thank you for bringing me here."

Roarke stepped closer, his presence behind me warm and inviting. "You're welcome, Milly. I'll happily take you wherever you want to go."

I turned away from the table, the thought of Roarke's unlimited magic filling my mind. "What *will* happen if we combine our magic?"

His eyes sparked with excitement. "You should feel the connection between us deepen, and your well of magic will grow. After that it shouldn't feel any different than when you use your magic in the real world. But here, like me, you'll only need to think of where you want to go and what you want to do. No spells required."

I looked around the tomb and felt nothing but truth in his words. This amazing life could be mine, and all I had to do was trust him. But in this moment, I still wasn't sure if I did. Or perhaps it was myself I didn't trust—I really couldn't tell. All I knew was that I needed more time.

"I'm sorry. I'm just not ready yet."

Lying awake back in my bed, I stared at the plaster ceiling, the missing flakes reminding me of all the real-world chores I needed to get done. Today my plan was to winterize the rest of the garden beds and restock my candles and creams. They'd provide a good substitute for the lack of vegetables I'd have in the final days of the farmers market this year. Unfortunately, chores be damned, all I could think about was him.

I writhed under the sheet, recalling the mystical, foreign places we'd visited so far. The once-in-a-lifetime things I'd learned. And most importantly, the surge of energy that filled my body when we almost joined our magic. For that brief moment, it was beyond anything I'd ever experienced before. But despite my grounding and truth spells and how our magic felt together, I had to admit I was still a little unsure. It wasn't as if I thought Roarke was lying to me, but I couldn't help feeling there was something more to his magic. I just didn't know what. And maybe that was it. The draw of it all. Maybe it was the mystery that called to my witch's soul. Something I needed to discover—about him *and* myself.

Jenks meowed from the kitchen, breaking my internal debate.

"Good morning, sweet boy. Are you ready for your breakfast?"

I pulled the quilt from my bed, wrapped it around my shoulders, and padded to the stove. The embers in the kitchen hearth still burned bright, and a plate of bacon and a slice of the raisin-cinnamon bread I baked last week sounded divine.

I set the kettle on the burner next to the pan and scooped out a tablespoon of my peppermint tea. The minty aroma swirled my senses, bringing with it a fresh wave of peace.

"Looks like today's the last day we'll get to play in the garden. Are you up for a few hours of work in the chilly morning air?"

Jenks excitedly rubbed himself around my ankles, providing his response.

"Good. I'm looking forward to it too."

Instinctively, I knew while my mind could float through the dreamscape every night, my body still needed to stay grounded in this world. The house, garden, and the life Mama and I created here meant so much to me. It was branded on my very soul. I learned about my magic here, how to hone my skills to provide for anything I'd need in life… except when it came to love.

It was the one spell we weren't allowed to cast. Love came from a source all its own, and no number of spells or manipulation could alter its true course. I wondered now if my ability to see and connect with the Weaver came from a completely different type of magic beyond either of our control. Perhaps we *were* meant for each other.

I turned away from the stove and lost myself in a dream of my own.

Roarke's hands roamed across my skin, eliciting goose bumps wherever he touched. Rolling my neck to the side, I could feel his lips press warmly against my throat, licking upward to my jawline and finishing at my lips with a passionate kiss. It was as if the goddess was showing me these things were finally possible—that I was destined for love with the man of my dreams.

Bacon sizzled in the pan, pulling my attention back to the real world. Smoke filled the air, and the stench of burned meat wrinkled my nose.

"Sorry, Jenks." I apologized and snatched the pan from the burner, noting the hiss and growl coming from my familiar. "Don't worry, baby. I can make another batch."

His iridescent amber eyes lingered on the smoke, his growl turning vicious as he bared his teeth.

8

I WASN'T ONE TO DISCOUNT AN OMEN, but I couldn't find anything in the smoke that should have triggered Jenks the way it did.

I cleaned up the kitchen, frustrated I'd ruined our breakfast and even more perturbed I was back to the push and pull of questioning myself again. Everything I felt for Roarke seemed natural but also not. I needed to get outside and bury my hands in the dirt. A witch had to stay grounded in order to connect with her magic, and maybe I was spending too much time with my head in the clouds.

Pulling on my boots, I grabbed my pruners and trowel from the bench near the door and burst out onto the back porch. Tilting my face to the sun, I relished in the tiniest amount of warmth it offered, fighting its way to warm my chilled bones. Following the stone path to the shed, I loaded the rake and bucket into the wheelbarrow and rolled it to the nearest bed. I needed to dig up the last of the root vegetables and harvest any remaining tomatoes and zucchini on the vines. Then it was time to put the earth to rest. And hopefully bury my fears and doubts alongside the dormant roots as well.

I had cared for this garden almost every day of my nineteen years, its bounty a blessing and a gift from my mother. Again, my connection to this place—to this land and the surrounding forest—was a part of my very being. A part of who I was at my very core. But for the first time, I wondered if that was a problem.

Could my earthbound magic be too much of a pull to provide the balance the Weaver needed? Based in the stars, his magic was influenced by the element of air. But even as a little girl, I never did like the wind.

I shoved my trowel into the dirt, questioning if the Weaver had made a mistake. Was I really powerful enough to be his queen? I swallowed past the lump in my throat, frustrated by my timid heart. Never once had I questioned my power before. Mama always made sure of that.

"Milly, the goddess resides inside us all. All you need to do is open your heart and embrace the power within."

The ritual of claiming your power marked an important point in any young witch's life. My mother's words were all it took for me to embrace my magic that long-ago night. And being raised a solitary witch meant I didn't need an elaborate celebration or over-the-top ceremony. Just an intimate ritual where I internally accepted who I was and acknowledged all I could become. Marked by a blessing from the goddess, I chose my path and was granted access to my hereditary magic and the constant energy provided by our land.

With my fingers buried in that same soil, I let the cold earth seep through my gloves, nipping at my fingertips as I loosened the bulbs of garlic. With a firm pull, the tubers came free, revealing a clump of at least four cloves. In ancient times, garlic was considered a source of great strength and could be used to treat infections if other medicines weren't readily available. And working with it now, I felt stronger.

Shaking the dirt loose, I laid the first of the vegetable in my basket and moved down the line. I had to stay strong and stop second-guessing myself at every turn. If the Weaver chose me, I'd already been found worthy.

I looked at my hands and removed my gloves. Pressing my palms against the frigid dirt, I closed my eyes. Stars flickered behind my lids, and I felt my magic rise. Warmth radiated from my fingers, thawing the ground and also my heart. I opened my eyes and gasped. My entire bed was in full bloom again. Garlic, potatoes, cosmos, and peonies, all flowering and ready for a second harvest. But as I pulled my hands away, the energy left me. Forcing the flowers and vegetables back to rest once more.

"Every Weaver has to have a partner to balance out their magic. If not, it creates an imbalance that can be felt in the real world. And I shouldn't have to tell you that any imbalance in nature is not a good thing." I stared at the dormant bed, recalling the Weaver's words. And for some reason, it made me sad.

Jenks bumped my side and meowed, bringing me back to myself.

"Thanks, buddy. You're right. I need to focus and finish the job."

Pulling myself together, I worked for the rest of the day, harvesting and mulching the vegetable beds. Now, with my stores full and the sun beginning its descent, I thought about the night ahead. Where would we go next? Again, the possibilities overwhelmed me as I headed to the shower, needing time to think.

Refreshed, I stoked the fire and set my tray of food on the coffee table, sinking down onto the couch. My pasta, salad, bread, and wine smelled and looked delicious. I couldn't wait to dig in. It was one of the comfort meals Mama always made, and even now, it was working its magic. I suddenly knew exactly where I wanted to go.

I finished my meal, enjoying Jenks's company next to the crackling fire, then cleaned the kitchen and prepared for bed. It was my goal to see if I could affect more of the dreamscape tonight with my own magic. From changing my clothes to where we visited, I wanted to assess my control.

Slipping beneath the covers, I settled us both in, petting Jenks as he nestled beside me. "Don't worry, sweet boy. I'll be fine." And I knew I would.

Closing my eyes, I focused on where I wanted to go and woke with a smile.

A warm wind brushed my cheeks, and it felt amazing.

"Good evening, Milly. I see you've already begun to test things for yourself."

Roarke's voice tugged at my heart. I opened my eyes, thrilled to see rolling vineyards and a Tuscan villa standing in the distance, just as I'd planned. It's square stone façade and manicured courtyard looked exactly like every picture I'd ever seen.

"I've always wanted to come here, and it doesn't disappoint." I wrapped my arms around my middle, noting the red floral button-up dress I had planned to wear already in place.

"Well, your magic worked perfectly, and you look absolutely beautiful tonight." Roarke took my hand. "Shall we?"

I dipped my head, not sure what he had in mind but ready to experience it all.

We walked through the vineyard rows in silence, taking in the splendor hand in hand. Plump purple grapes hung thick on the vines, while bright-green leaves blew gently in the wind.

Nearing the villa, I pulled Roarke to a stop. "I want to try something if that's okay?"

The Weaver smiled. "Be my guest."

Concentrating, I let my magic rise to the surface and sent my thoughts into the cosmos. Roarke chuckled beside me, and I opened my eyes to a little red corvette. It was exactly the type of car I imagined touring the countryside in. Top down, wind in my hair, exploring the rolling hills of Tuscany.

"Shall we?" I repeated his words.

Jumping in the car, Roarke guided us down main streets and through back roads for the rest of the day, stopping whenever I wanted to take in the scenery. Our last break involved a picnic lunch in the middle of a field, including a visit from a curious cow.

"This has been fantastic." I lifted my glass of Chianti. "Salute."

"Salute," Roarke answered, tipping his glass toward mine. With a wave of his hand, the field transformed, taking my breath away.

A circle of meadow and blooming wildflowers surrounded us, instantly reminding me of a scene from a movie. Lying back, I basked in the Tuscan sun, smiling like a fool. "This is beautiful too." My eyes met his as he lay down beside me.

"I thought we could rest here for a bit before heading back to the villa for dinner."

I leaned up on my elbow. "That sounds lovely. But is there something at the villa we need to do?"

"No. I just thought with this being your first planned trip, you'd want to make the most of it." He plucked a viola from the grass between us and tucked it behind my ear.

Lying back, I folded my hands atop my stomach and stared at the puffy white clouds above me. I'd never felt like this before. So free. So... *wild.* Without thinking, I reached out my hand and found his waiting beside me. A slow grin overtook my lips, but I kept my eyes locked on the sky.

Time seemed to move differently in the dreamscape. We lay in the meadow, talking, laughing, and holding hands, for what felt like only a few minutes. But in reality, hours had passed.

"Are you ready for dinner?" Roarke asked.

"Yes. And you said we'd be dining back at the villa, right?"

"That's right. Unless there's somewhere else you'd like to go." Roarke pulled me upright, and the meadow disappeared, replaced by the original field. Cows meandered in the distance, and the little red corvette still sat beside the road.

"No. This day has been perfect, and I'd love to finish it with dinner there." I straightened my dress and slipped back into my oat-colored flats as bells rang in the distance, pulling my eyes toward the sky.

"It's time to head back." Roarke took my hand and led me to the car, opening my door like a perfect gentleman.

"Where are those bells coming from?" I asked.

Roarke's eyes drifted to the city below. "Do you know most modern clocks run on French time?"

I shook my head, not clear where this conversation was going.

"There's only one clock in the world that runs on Italian time, and it's in the Duomo right down there." He pointed down the hill to the heart of Florence.

"Wow. That's… interesting." I climbed into the passenger seat as the engine roared to life.

"It is actually. The clock has a spiral of Roman numerals on it that run backward, or counterclockwise, ending at the bottom with the number twenty-four."

"Really?" I was intrigued. "So midnight is marked at the bottom of the clock instead of the top?"

"No. That's what's so unique. The hand moves in reverse like a shadow of a sundial, counting down the hours of the day. Twenty-four marks the hour when the sun sets, not midnight."

I peered past Roarke's shoulder, looking down at the city, and imagined the clock sitting in the cathedral far below.

"Its purpose was to warn the farmers and workers of the 1400s to end their day and get back inside the walls of the city before the gates closed. They still adjust it today, resetting it each week so the hour of sunset is correct throughout the year." Roarke concluded as we pulled up to the villa.

I sat still, staring at this man and wondering what other mysteries he'd learned throughout his life. "How old are you, Roarke?" The question slid off my tongue before I could stop it.

"To your eyes, twenty-three."

I let his words sink in, noticing the twitch in his jaw. "But you weren't the Weaver during the time of the pharaohs, right?" I teased, remembering what he'd mentioned when we were back in Egypt.

"That's right." Stepping around the car, he opened my door and offered his hand. "Shall we? Dinner awaits."

And just like that, time moved on.

9

"THIS IS FANTASTIC."

I finished off my last bite of bruschetta, which I now knew was called fettunta in this part of the country. The freshly toasted Tuscan bread was generously rubbed with garlic and lavishly drizzled with green olive oil then sparingly sprinkled with salt. I licked my lips, savoring the flavors, excited to be experiencing all this for real instead of just reading about it in books.

Growing up on my own, the only adventures I had were thanks to the images and words of others—Keelyn at one point calling me a modern-day savant. Knowing the meaning, I laughed at the word but still didn't think it applied to me.

"Did you know that each Italian region has their own distinct dishes?" Roarke asked midbite, which of course I did not.

My eyes widened as a large bowl of panzanella salad—made with day-old bread, tomatoes, onion, basil, olive oil, and balsamic vinegar—was set between us on the table. I dished out two servings for both of us to share.

"It's true. So much so that some argue there isn't really such a thing as *Italian* food but rather Sicilian or Venetian or of course, my favorite now, Tuscan food." He smiled and winked, then took a bite of the stale bread that accompanied our meal. "Much like this bread, Tuscan cuisine is inspired by traditional 'peasant food' from the surrounding farming regions. The simple, rustic ingredients might have humble roots but were cherished and nurtured, and nothing was ever thrown away."

I took another sip of wine, swallowing my first bite. "Well, that's something I can certainly appreciate. I try to use everything my garden produces and know how to layer flavor with just the right spice or herb."

Roarke set down his fork. "That's something I'd very much like to see."

I smiled but shook my head. "What do you mean?"

"I'd like to see you cook."

"Um..." I stammered. "I thought we couldn't interact in the real world?"

"We can't, but obviously, what *we* experience in the dreamscape is as close to real as anyone can get. You could cook for me at my cabin." He shrugged, digging back into his meal.

Cook for him in the dreamscape in his secret home in the middle of the woods? I shoveled another forkful of food into my mouth, buying me some time to answer. Admittedly, I'd been falling for the Weaver since I first saw him in my dreams. But now he was becoming a major part of my life, and the potential to deepen our connection was as real as the moon in the sky.

A shooting star streaked overhead, and I chuckled to myself. My heart was that star—constantly racing ahead and pulling me along in its wake.

I took another sip of wine and replied, "I would be happy to cook for you. Just name the time and date."

"Tomorrow night as soon as you fall asleep."

I swallowed past a lump in my throat that was definitely not the bread. Sitting back, I placed my napkin across my plate. "Any requests?" I tried to be brave, though my insides were a muddled mess.

"Not really. Surprise me." Roarke, too, had finished his meal and stood up from the table. "This has been a wonderful evening, Milly, but it's time we return."

I placed my hand in his, steadying my wobbly knees and fluttering heart as he helped me from my chair. We walked down the cobblestone path hand in hand, nearing my dream car again.

"Since you brought all this into existence, you'll need to be the one to send it back."

Panicked and unsure of what to do, I stumbled over my words. "Send it back... to where? I simply thought it into the dream like you told me I could."

"That's right. And now you just need to think it gone."

Again, I closed my eyes but lifted a lid to confirm I was doing it right. I imagined the parking lot empty and smiled when Roarke exhaled and squeezed my hand.

"See, I told you it would be easy to use your magic here."

I opened my eyes, satisfied as he pulled me forward, ready to take us back to reality. But as I looked behind me, I could swear I saw smoke in the distance, dancing on the wind.

Waking in bed alone, I didn't feel Jenks's weight upon the covers. "Jenks? Are you okay, sweet boy? Where are you?" A scuffle in the back room brought me upright, my eyes straining to adjust in the dark. "Come back to bed, buddy. I need you."

Light footsteps padded into the room, followed by a sweet meow. Jenks jumped up onto the bed, settling on top of my chest as I lay back down.

"Hi there," I whispered, stroking his fur.

Between the purring and his grounding energy, my familiar had me relaxed and back to sleep within minutes—and thankfully without any further dreams. With my adventures over for the night, I slept like a baby… until the next morning when I saw the news.

Pictures of a burned-out vineyard flashed on the TV as a reporter read something off her paper about a freak lightning storm hitting the area.

My cup crashed to the floor, spilling my morning tea. "No, no, no. This cannot be happening." Desperate to learn more, I searched for the remote. But by the time I raised the volume, the story had passed. "Dammit!" I tossed the thing back onto the couch, slamming the cushions beside me.

I'd had prophetic dreams in the past, dreaming of something that came true the next day. But not like this. It couldn't be. The night Roarke and I just shared in Italy couldn't possibly have anything to do with this. Could it?

I yanked on my boots, pulling them snug beneath my plain housedress, then grabbed a sweater from the hook by the door. I needed to see if Keelyn had found any other books that mentioned the Weaver and get back to my research as initially planned.

I started down the path that would lead me to town, noting the various animals scurrying throughout the woods. Squirrels rushed to add to their winter stockpiles, while bright-red cardinals flitted among the trees. My forest was alive no matter what time of year it was.

"Milly, if you're ever unsure, you can always look to the trees. Animals know when there is danger about, so all you need to do is open your eyes and watch for their signs."

Mama's words floated through my mind like a wisp of wind, bringing me back to balance with a single gust. While my imagination might be on high alert, there was no danger here.

Slowing to a comfortable pace, I meandered down the path, reaching the library a little after nine.

"Hi, Milly. It's good to see you again so soon. I didn't expect you until later in the week."

I was surprised by Keelyn's words. "You were expecting me?"

[78]

Her kind smile made her ice-blue eyes sparkle as if they were hiding a secret. "Yes, well, since you asked me to do a little more digging on any books containing the word *weaver*, I figured you'd be back to check on my progress."

Great! We were on the same page. "Did you find anything?" My words came out too loud, a man in the corner shushing me.

Keelyn laughed under her breath. "Not yet, but I haven't stopped looking. Why don't you come by the house on Thursday for book club? I'll hopefully have something for you by then."

I looked around the library, nervous at the idea of being around so many people. Thankfully, Keelyn knew me all too well.

"Don't worry. There won't be a lot of people there this week. We've just finished a book not many of us liked, so I don't expect too many readers to stop by."

My heart returned to a normal pace, and I nodded my agreement.

"Fantastic! I'll be sure to prepare some of my yogurt cakes using the remaining currants I have from last year."

"Sounds good. I'll see you then." I gave Keelyn a small wave goodbye, proud of myself for accepting her invitation, then left the library with food on my mind. I still had to plan for the dinner I was supposed to cook Roarke tonight but had no idea how to begin.

Would the ingredients I wanted to use just appear at his cabin, or would he provide the items he wanted me to cook?

"Dammit, I should have asked more questions," I reprimanded myself.

"What's that now? For once, Keelyn didn't have the answers you seek?" A deep voice sounded from over my shoulder, and I spun around.

Peter O'Toolle was strolling down the sidewalk, his light-brown hair almost as disheveled as I'd left it in the barn all those years ago.

"Hello, Peter. How are you?" I asked plainly.

"I'm good, Milly. How are you?" His eyes dipped to the concrete, staring at his feet as they always did.

I studied him, realizing that seeing him now didn't have the same effect on me as it usually did. Being with Roarke had changed me already. I felt like a woman. Almost a queen.

I lifted my head and met his stare, emboldened by a confidence I rarely felt around others. "Did you need something?" I asked, not intending to be rude but honestly wondering what he was doing here in the middle of the day.

"No. I'm just waiting for Jess." He tipped his chin toward the library's front door.

Jessica Craven was the second girl Peter slept with when we were younger and had gone on to become his wife.

"We're having a baby." He shuffled his feet. "She's looking for some pregnancy books inside."

The words were like a blow to my chest, a hard thud cracking a rib. I wasn't jealous, but one thought blasted through my head: *Being the Weaver's queen, will I ever have the chance to have kids?*

"Milly, are you okay?" Peter's voice broke through my shock.

I shook my head, swallowing my surprise, and searched for the proper words. "Yes. Sorry, I'm fine. Congratulations, Peter." I smiled as genuinely as I could, then raced away down the street.

I skipped the grocery store, returning home at a breakneck pace, and flopped down onto my bed. I'd never given much thought to kids, but as a hereditary witch, it was obviously an expected thing. Mothers were meant to pass their magic on to their children.

Jenks jumped up beside me, nudging my cheek with his little head.

"I'm okay, buddy. Just having a rough day."

My familiar continued to do his job, weaving his special energy into my heart and soul. It wasn't that I was sad about Peter's news. It just made me think. I'd fallen so hard for Roarke already, given our mystical situation, but I never considered how his magic would affect me in the real world.

I lifted my head, catching sight of something lying on my pillow. A viola.

The viola from the meadow that he'd placed behind my ear. It was here in my room, leaving me with even more questions than when my day began. Between the Weaver's confusing appearance in my bedroom, the fire in Italy, and now this—

The delicate flower was still soft in my hand, reminding me again of how special our time together was. I opened the wooden box on my altar and placed it inside. I'd lived my life so reserved. So focused and yet completely content. But looking around the room, I found myself wanting. There was nothing wrong with the wooden desk sitting in the corner or the six-drawer dresser Mama had handed down to me. But I couldn't deny my heart any longer—I wanted more.

Resolved, I showered off the dirt of the day and dressed for our dinner.

10

"*Mmm*... THIS SMELLS DELICIOUS." ROARKE sniffed the steam rising from my pot of clams.

"Thank you. I've decided to honor my hometown and make clams three ways: on the half shell, clam chowder, and clam cakes over rice pilaf with a side of fresh asparagus for the main course."

"Damn, Milly, you really do know how to cook."

Roarke had been waiting for me in his hidden forest, greeting me with a friendly wave and a big smile as soon as I'd fallen asleep. The ingredients I needed came to me inside his cabin the moment I gave thought to my culinary plans.

"Mama taught me well." I threw in a pinch of salt and walked away from the stove. "Can I ask you something?"

"Of course. Anything you'd like."

"This morning I woke up to a news report about a vineyard in Italy burning to the ground. And I think I saw smoke in the dreamscape right before we left last night." I moved closer to the fireplace. "I want to know how your magic affects the real world."

Roarke stood still, crossing his arms over his chest.

"I guess what I'm asking is... did the vineyard we visited in Tuscany burn up because of us?"

With a deep sigh, Roarke moved to the couch. "Milly, come sit with me." He held out a hand, and I took a seat beside him. "Yes, there are things that happen in the dreamscape that also take place in the real world, providing the balance required. However, sometimes the things that happen there *are* just dreams. And in this case, a nightmare it seems."

"Whose nightmare?"

"Whoever's dream it was." He shrugged. "It could have been the vineyard's owner, a disgruntled worker, or a paranoid tourist worried about his first vacation to Italy." He squeezed my hand. "Either way, it's nothing you need to worry about."

The clatter of boiling clams pulled me back to the kitchen. I stood over the pot, stirring and wondering if he was right. None of my earlier visits with the Weaver involved a nightmare of any kind, but it would be silly to think they never would. We all had nightmares lying in wait within our psyche.

I started to lift the clams out of the pot but had another thought. According to Roarke, I didn't really need to be doing any of this. I could simply focus my magic to complete our meal exactly the way I envisioned it.

I pictured the clams lying open in a bowl of ice, then the chowder peppered and dished into two bowls with accompanying plates of clam cakes, rice, and asparagus prepared beside them.

Turning to the table, I smiled. "Dinner is served."

Roarke's hearty laugh filled the cabin. "There you go! Way to use your magic, Milly. And just in time... I'm starving!"

I untied the apron from around my waist and joined Roarke at the table. I needed time to process what he said, but I wasn't about to ruin our meal. "I hope you like everything."

Roarke slid out my chair, whispering in my ear, "I have no doubt I'll love it all."

A chill shivered up my spine as I scooted forward.

Roarke settled across from me at the table, winking as he began to enjoy his meal. I was never one to think the act of eating was sexy, but seeing him slip the clams onto his tongue and watching as he licked his lips caused a flush to run through me. My body felt like it had that day in the barn with Peter, and suddenly, I didn't have anything else to say. I lifted a spoonful of chowder to my lips, blowing on it to bring the temperature down, when I caught the Weaver's eyes. He was staring at me as if I were part of the meal.

I lowered my spoon. "Is something wrong?"

A smile pulled at his lips, and he shook his head. "Milly, when you're here, there's absolutely nothing wrong in my world."

I couldn't stop the blush that heated my cheeks. "May I ask you another question?"

"Of course." He nodded and slurped down another clam.

"From some of the things you say, I assume you've been watching me for a while. How long, exactly, before I saw you in my dreams?"

Roarke set down his fork, placing a hand on either side of his plate. "Milly, I haven't been spying on you if that's what you're thinking. That's not how this works." He chuckled. "Once I became the Weaver, my magic instinctively began to search for my queen. I've appeared to multiple witches throughout time, but until I found the one powerful enough to see me in return, I had no way of pinpointing who you were. However, the longing to connect with my mate was always there, pulling at my soul."

"I'm sorry... Did you say *mate*?"

Roarke laughed. "I did, but it's not as barbaric as it sounds."

Queen. Partner. Companion. Mate..... He kept dropping these words, and all were great to hear, but I wasn't sure what they meant for me.

I thought about Peter and Jess.

"What does that mean exactly? Are we now bound to one another forever? Like a husband and wife?" I stuffed a clam cake in my mouth, forcing myself to stop talking.

Roarke sat silent until I looked up and met his eyes. "What we are to each other goes far beyond husband and wife. We are eternally linked. Can't you feel it?"

I swallowed hard and took a sip of water, hoping to dowse the emotions rising inside me. Roarke's words continued to drudge up thoughts and desires I'd secretly held inside for so very long. To love someone and to be loved in return. But that was the one word he had yet to use.

Closing my eyes, I searched for the link he described—a mark on my soul that belonged distinctly to him. A warm feeling flared in my gut, burning like wildfire and spreading throughout my veins. At its source pulsed an intimate beat, banging against my insides like the call of a ritual drum. My head lolled to the side, and I lost myself to its rhythm. Strong hands landed on my shoulders, followed by the trail of his swiping fingers down the side of my neck.

"Do you feel it, Milly? How our magic reacts to one another?"

My eyes popped open, reality slamming into me. What if this feeling *was* only due to our magic and nothing else? Sure, he'd called me his queen, his mate, but he'd called us partners as well. And in this moment, I felt like a fool, realizing that's all we might be—business partners.

I pulled away and excused myself from the table. Walking outside onto the back deck, I looked to the sky and tried to lose myself in the stars. Shimmering high above me, the black canvas of night held its usual masterpiece painted in blues, purples, and pinks. But the longer I stared, the more the stars swirled together, muddling my hopes and dreams.

The glass door slid open behind me, and Roarke's low voice drifted to my ears. "Are you all right?"

I wrapped my arms around my stomach and answered honestly. "I'm not sure."

He eased up behind me, this time keeping his hands to himself. My heart clenched at the loss.

"Do you want to come back inside and talk about it?" He paused. "I'm sorry I upset you."

I looked out over the water, trying to find the words to explain, but all the ones creeping onto my tongue were too embarrassing to say. "It's okay. You didn't do anything wrong."

And he didn't. These issues were mine and mine alone.

"Okay. Then I'll give you some time while I go finish your deliciously magical meal."

His response pulled a bark of laughter out of me, and I realized what a gift I'd been given. Whether love was truly a part of it or not, I'd been deemed a powerful witch—one strong enough to join the Weaver in this amazing world.

Not one to brood or dwell, I turned to follow him back inside. "I'm ready to join you now." The words carried a double meaning, my heart hardening against them.

We finished the meal in amicable silence, broken only by Roarke's praises in regard to my cooking. "Honestly, Milly, these are the most delicious clams I've ever tasted. What's your secret?"

"Just the right amount of spice and love." I shrugged, needing to keep some things to myself.

"Well, you've created the perfect balance." He pushed back his plate and tossed his napkin down beside it. "What do you want to do for the rest of the evening? Any particular adventure piquing your interest?"

Again, I thought through the unlimited options but refused to become overwhelmed. "I want to go back to Tuscany and check on that vineyard."

Roarke stopped midsip, his glass of Sauvignon Blanc stalling in the air. "Are you sure? I already explained the fire was just part of a dream." He chucked back the final gulp of wine, his jaw twitching as he swallowed.

I rose from my chair to clear the dishes, the mundane task buying me some time.

"Yes, well, I'd still like to see it for myself." I lowered my plate into the sink, realizing how silly it was to be doing dishes in the Weaver's home. Instead, I imagined the table and kitchen clean, then stood awestruck when my will was immediately done.

The fire popped behind me, and I turned to find Roarke ready, pulling on his cloak. "Then we shall go so you can see for yourself."

"Thank you, and I'm sorry. It's not that I don't trust you, but I've always been taught to follow my gut." I conjured a sweater of my own, questioning my words as I pushed my arms through the sleeves. If I did trust him, then why was I insisting we go? I shook my head and followed him out into the woods.

With a wave of his hand, a slice appeared, and we stepped through without delay.

The vineyard looked the same, and the beautiful stone winery still stood in front of us, unharmed.

"See, everything is good," Roarke declared.

I turned back to the rows of grapes behind us, falling in waves as they led my eyes down the hill. "Yes, and I'm so relieved. Thank you for bringing me back."

"Your wish is my command." He repeated the same words he'd used before. "Where do you want to go now? Since we're back in Italy, would you like to see Lake Garda? It's considered one of the most beautiful places in the country. Or perhaps Positano on the Amalfi Coast? Or how about the Island of Capri or Venice or Sorrento on the Bay of Naples? Or we could pay a quick visit to Rome. What do you think?"

I thought my head might explode from all the choices, once again overwhelmed despite my best efforts. "If it's all right with you, I'd like to go down into town. Maybe see that special clock in the Duomo of Florence?"

Roarke stood still with his head cocked as if listening to the wind. "Actually, I don't like to visit the same area twice within such close timing. So it would probably be best if we picked another place."

The hairs on the back of my neck stood on end as a waft of charred wood drifted to my nose. I wondered then just whose dream this was. If Roarke himself was shaping the scene, it meant he was purposely lying to me.

I took one last look at the villa, pinpointing smoke rising from a chimney and inhaled deeply. Catching the aroma of food being cooked, I closed my eyes and let my magic rise to the surface, searching for the truth. I wasn't entirely sure if what I was seeing was real or not, but regardless, Roarke had brought me here, exactly like I asked. And for now... that was enough.

I placed my hand in his, my heart and mind again *somewhat* at ease.

11

I WIPED MY BROW, THANKFUL FOR THE sun in the sky as I pressed in the final plant of my cold-weather herbs. The sharp scent of rosemary pierced my nose, and I smiled as Jenks chased another field mouse across the yard. Spending the day with my hands in the dirt was a welcome reprieve as I contemplated what to do.

Obviously, I'd have to make a decision soon about joining the Weaver.

"Milly, there's a time in every witch's life when a hard choice has to be made. Just be brave, and your magic will see you through."

I tilted my face to the sun, letting its warm rays heat my cheeks. Mama's lessons always rang true exactly when I needed them, but more than anything, I wished she was here.

Losing myself in the fantasy of books was how I'd spent most of my time after she was gone. Flying high on a dragon's back with a handsome knight holding me tight or exploring the deep sea with a roguish and fearless captain were the only experiences with men I had to draw on… besides Peter, of course—the fantasy outweighing reality. And now spending time with Roarke had me yearning for Mama's guidance more than ever.

Standing and smoothing my apron, I gathered my basket of basil, oregano, parsley, and thyme and returned to the house. The chill of the stone floor in the back room penetrated my boots even as the sun still warmed my back. Fall was almost upon us, and the leaves on the trees would start changing soon enough. This was my favorite time of year, and the timing of the Weaver's presence—*Roarke's* presence—somehow felt less than ironic. The turning of the wheel was spinning toward the Witches New Year, and I wondered how different my life would be the next time Mabon, Samhain, and Yule came around.

As my final task from the garden this year, I sorted the herbs and bound them with twine, hanging them from the rafters to dry. Even separate from their main, life-giving plant, they still carried magic inside them with a new purpose to serve.

"Just be brave…"

I shook my head. I wasn't sure if I could.

With a final touch to their dried stalks, I turned off the light and plunged the herbs into their next phase of life… a life from death.

I paced the hardwood floor the same way my mom did—in my bare feet, walking until my heels were almost raw. Unable to sleep, I tossed over everything in my mind. Roarke had whisked me away to Venice after I hadn't responded in the vineyard, and while the beauty and grandeur was something I'd never forget, so was the feeling he was still hiding something from me.

I needed to get back to my research and hoped by Thursday Keelyn would have found something of use. I looked at the clock on the wall, its gold hands creeping their way through the night, and thought about what I could do since I wouldn't be going back to bed anytime soon.

Jenks was curled up on my mattress, nestled in the blankets and purring soundly. I left the bedroom, gently pulling the door closed behind me. I stoked the fire next, needing its warmth to thaw my chilled bones, then filled the kettle, longing for some tea. September might be the first month of fall, but here in Rhode Island, the temperatures could dip toward freezing in the blink of an eye. With my garden beds already harvested and winterized, I found myself somewhat at a loss. And that was annoying.

During the past six years, I had occupied myself with chores and crafts from dawn till dusk. So why were things different now? *You know why*, I told myself. Because nothing could compare to spending time with Roarke in the dreamscape. Every dream I'd ever had was now a reality, and I wanted more.

I chose not to return to his cabin after Venice, ending our evening early instead. He didn't question me, but I suddenly wondered if he could have denied my choice, keeping me there against my will. It was something I'd have to ask the next time I saw him for sure.

The soft chimes of the clock rang three times, indicating it was three in the morning. All my creams and candles had been prepared, and my stores were stocked for the next farmers market, so I clicked on the reading light above the couch and pulled a book from a nearby shelf. Preparing my tea once the kettle whistled, I sat down and forced myself to relax.

The words on the page were familiar and worn. Dragons soared through the air with knights on their backs, and as usual, I imagined myself one of them. I slammed the book shut, reprimanding myself for not enjoying the gift I'd been given. Roarke needed me, so why did I continue to think something bad was going on? Again, perhaps the doubts stemmed from within myself. This new life was almost too good to be true, and I wondered if that had anything to do with my concerns.

"Milly, if something seems too good to be true, it usually is."

Mama's words knocked around in my head as my heart thumped heavily against my ribs. *This is ridiculous!* I jumped up from the couch, the book falling with a thud to the floor. Pacing again, I had to get my thoughts and fears under control.

Lighting a stick of Nag Champa, I lay on the couch and pulled my favorite afghan up to my chin. The Weaver might hold dominion over my dreams, but I was still a powerful witch in my own right.

Goddess of night, hear my plea. Shroud me from the one who sees. Let me walk within my dreams, shielded and alone. So mote it be.

I cast the spell into the darkness and closed my eyes, praying it would work. I needed to experience the dreamscape without Roarke hovering nearby if I was ever going to trust myself in his world or with him.

A hushed wind greeted me, and I instantly knew where I was. Roarke's hidden forest spread out around me, sleeping in silence as if it were resting, awaiting his return.

I crept down the tree-lined path toward his cabin, nervous he would catch me with every step. Smoke roiled from the chimney as the path opened up, revealing his hidden home, welcoming as ever. I stopped before reaching the front door, veering around to the lake instead.

The dark water was as calm and smooth as glass, and I wished my heart could be the same. But instead it was racing a mile a minute, beating wildly and sparking my fears in vibrant color. I had no idea what I should be looking for in order to ease my nerves. Did I really think the Weaver was hiding something, or was I simply too scared to share a part of myself with someone else after all this time? I looked down at my white-knuckled grip on the railing and admitted I was terrified to let go. Terrified I might turn around and find Roarke disappointed in me. Terrified to fully access all the unlimited power he was offering. But mostly, terrified to fully trust the Weaver with my heart.

I forced my fingers open and flung them out wide. Light burst forth all around me, blanketing the night in a fresh layer of day. Birds began to chirp in the distance, the trees stretching awake in an early morning breeze.

"Milly, is that you? What are you doing here?" Roarke came to stand behind me, hesitating when I didn't turn around.

"I have so many questions, but let's start with the obvious one. Will I ever be able to enter the dreamscape without you now?"

A slight inhale betrayed Roarke's shock. "Is that what you want? To be here without me?"

Disappointment rang in his voice like the bottom note of an organ at church, resonating deep within the cavity of my chest.

"I don't know," I admitted. "I'm just struggling to figure out all the *rules*."

Roarke's strong hand slid into mine. "Come inside, Milly, and I'll put on some tea."

I pulled my hand away. "No thank you." For the first time in my life, I didn't think tea would help. I chuckled under my breath, wondering what my mother would think.

"Then how about some coffee while we talk this out?"

I finally turned to face him, taking in his ruffled dark hair and sexy scruff. And if I were being honest, I wanted to jump into his arms and crush my mouth to his. I didn't want coffee or any other beverage. I only wanted to drink him in, but I still had questions. So denying myself another dream, I followed him back inside.

"Tea sounds great," I stated flatly.

12

I SAT ON ROARKE'S COUCH, REVELING IN the sweet taste of peppermint against my tongue. I'd almost done the most mortifying thing and still wondered if I'd regret it if I *had* followed my heart instead of my head.

Roarke poured himself a cup of tea and sat down beside me. "Tell me your concerns, Milly, and I'll try to answer them the best I can."

I swallowed a mouthful of the hot liquid, accepting the burn all the way down my throat. I wasn't sure how to express my concerns or really what they even were... I just knew I still had doubts. Doubts if I could do this. Doubts about what it was we were doing at all. Doubts about his feelings for me.

"I'm not sure how to explain it. I just still don't understand how all this works."

Roarke set his cup on the glass coffee table and took both of my hands in his. "I'll try to lay it out chronologically and see if that helps." He smiled kindly. "When I turned twenty-three in my original life, the Weaver magic sparked inside me. My family comes from a long line of Weavers, and it was either me or my brother who was next in line, and it just happened to be me."

"Wait. What do you mean your original life?"

"Once you accept the position of Weaver, your lifespan changes. Slowing and stretching across all of time and space. I accepted the title over one hundred and seventy-five years ago."

I stared into his sparkling eyes, awestruck as I tried to imagine all he'd seen and lost.

"Since then I've served as the Weaver alone, always searching for my queen." He reached out, brushing a finger down my cheek.

"I thought you said your queen brings you the balance you need. So what did you do without me for the last hundred and seventy-five years?" I hated referring to myself like that. Like I was somehow important in the grand scheme of things.

"Yes, that's right. And if you haven't noticed, the world hasn't exactly been going great for a really long time."

My eyes widened. "You mean to say that if you'd found me earlier, the world itself would be in a better place?"

Roarke's lips tipped into a grin. "Yes, Milly, that's what I'm trying to say. The world at large… and my world too."

I pulled my hands from his. "See, this is part of what I don't understand!" I stood, needing to move while I worked through all the thoughts pounding in my head. "Every night I wake in the dreamscape where you and I basically take a magical vacation, ignoring anything and everything happening around us. And *that's* somehow supposed to help the real world?" I tossed my hands in the air. "I just don't get it!"

Roarke sighed. "Let me try to put it in witch's terms. You're familiar with the rule of three, yes?"

I nodded.

"Then think of it like that but times a billion. Every thought, promise, hope, and dream of all of the people in the world is cast into the dreamscape every night, and whatever they put out can be accessed by us. Then my magic—the Weaver's magic—without any effort from me, takes those hopes and dreams and molds them into something that can help that person. Like with the sphinx and the pharaoh, the Weaver of that time guided him to make a discovery that would change his life and the world. Like the rule of three, whatever energy a person casts into the dreamscape, be it positive or negative, can be returned a billionfold. It's up to us and our magic to bring balance to that."

His words sank like a stone in my gut, only to rise again on the back of my hopes and dreams. The Weaver magic was what affected the world, and we were simply its vessels. I was beginning to understand.

Though more questions lingered in the back of my mind— small questions that rose and popped, coming and going in the span of a heartbeat, then floating away like a bubble on the wind—I finally felt as though I might actually belong. My hereditary magic was what got me here, but if I chose to become the Weaver's queen, I'd be strong enough to effect real change in the world.

I sat back down with tears in my eyes. "Thank you for choosing me."

Roarke cupped my face, his thumb rubbing tiny circles across my cheek. "Milly, it's I who should be thanking you. I've been alone for so long, and, so excited to show you my world, I never considered it would be hard for you to accept. So thank you for your patience and for allowing me to explain."

Heat blossomed beneath my skin, starting under his thumb and spreading to every cell in my body. He was exactly like me. Alone for most of his life and putting on a brave face. Fighting past his shyness while still unsure. Forever hiding beneath that damn cloak, all the while waiting for me.

"I want to try something." I leaned forward, placing my forehead to his, our third eyes pressed together. "Will you allow me in? Will you allow me to see?" I guided my magic up to the point where our skin touched, hoping he'd say yes.

Roarke tensed but shifted his body closer, then closed his eyes. "Of course."

There was no need to speak my spell aloud, so with my eyes closed, I cast my desire into the ether without saying another word. Images flashed within my mind's eye. Pictures of a young Roarke and another boy running through a field—his brother. Their family gathered around a wooden table, laughing and breaking bread, happy and fulfilled. Starry skies, the likes of which I'd never seen, painting a map of all the different worlds available to his father, the Weaver before him. Then Roarke with his arms splayed wide, his chest bursting with cosmic magic as he was deemed the next in line.

Images morphed into emotions, and I began to *feel* what he'd endured over the last century. The void left by losing his family. The utter isolation of always being alone. The constant nagging that something was missing from his life. And the never-ending search for the one who would make him whole.

I pulled back, breaking our connection. He'd been laid bare before me and knew what I saw. The vulnerable expression on his face confirmed as much, and it broke my heart.

Emotions still raw, I simply asked, "Can you give me until tomorrow night?"

Roarke wiped the tears from his eyes and nodded slowly. "I'll be waiting."

I spent the day meditating, cooking, and playing with Jenks. Tonight was the new moon. While most people associated witches and their magic with the *full* moon instead, the dark moon offered a chance for a fresh start and to set new intentions, which was exactly what I planned to do.

Retrieving last month's moon water from the fridge, I added it to my bath. Steam rose in billowing wafts, the scent of mugwort, lavender, and patchouli oil filling the small room. The essential oils would boost my dream work, and the ritual bath would prepare my mind and body for the journey ahead. Sliding into the clawfoot tub, I set my intention as one of openness and magic and hoped the goddess would hear my plea. Water enveloped me, wrapping me in a cocoon as I sank below the surface, its fragrant warmth covering me from the tips of my toes to just under my chin.

I let myself drift off mentally, welcoming the goddess and any message she might have. I thought back over the past few months and everything that had happened with the Weaver so far, focusing on my intention to join him now. This was something I wanted, and my magic had proved strong enough so far, having called his attention to me in the first place.

Goddess of night, hear me now. I cleanse my body as part of our vow. Wash away all fear and doubt as I prepare to call on you, your faithful devout.

I inhaled deeply, welcoming the relaxing state of my ritual bath. With one hand between my legs and the other resting across my breasts, I drew the triangle of the sacred feminine, alternating positions as my hands slid up and down and across my skin.

"Maiden, Mother, Crone. Maiden, Mother, Crone." I repeated the call until my breasts heaved and goose bumps dotted my skin.

The goddess was here.

I pulled the plug, letting my doubts and fears swirl down the drain.

Striding to the back porch, I stood skyclad with my arms raised to the heavens above.

"Goddess, I ask that you hear my plea, shining your blessings down upon me. Grant me the magic I need to transform while maintaining my connection to all that's been born. From my ancestors flows the magic in me, protected and rooted so completely. This new phase is welcome and has begun. Show me your will, and it shall be done."

A warm breeze blew across my body as the goddess's words penetrated my mind.

"At the darkest time of night, there is a turning point. From darkness to light. From death to life. A journey completed, and a new journey begins. Behold! I am the Lady of Darkness, mother and grandmother. Hail to the Crone! Old yet young, Mother darksome and divine. As the wheel turns, we see birth, death, and rebirth and know from this that every end is a beginning. Maiden, Mother, Crone, I am all these and more. Whenever you have need, call upon me, and I will be there. I abide within you even at the darkest times. When there seems no single spark to warm you, I am she who is at the beginning and at the end of all time. Harm none and love all life. So mote it be."

"So mote it be," I repeated aloud as three chimes sounded in the back of my head. I knew now my magic was ready for the connection to be made.

Jenks followed me straight to bed, snuggling in as I flicked my wrist to stoke the fire again. It warmed my nakedness, and I squirmed beneath the blankets, preparing for sleep. Welcoming the goddess back into my heart, I was ready to meet Roarke and deliver my answer once and for all.

13

A COOL BREEZE BRUSHED MY SKIN, AND I wondered if I'd shown up in the dreamscape still as naked as I was in bed. Roarke said my clothes partly came from me, so I certainly expected to be covered when I arrived.

Looking down, I thankfully noted the ritual gown hanging from my frame. White panels draped my front and back, cinched by an ornate golden belt. My hair had gone straight, and a headpiece weighed heavy upon my brow. I beamed, happy with my chosen location. I imagined I looked like Anck-Su-Namun from the movie, an Egyptian princess ready to commit to her prince.

Footsteps sounded behind me. Then Roarke's voice was at my ear. "I never imagined I could be this lucky. You're a vision, Milly. Are you ready? You are my chosen, but the choice to join me is yours alone."

I swallowed and turned around. "I'm ready. And I *do* choose you."

He took my hands, emotions playing across his face. A twitch in my palm captured my attention. Magic pulsed in my veins, running like a river to where our skin connected, and I gasped. A tiny cosmos burst to life between our palms, encircling our hands as it shimmered and grew. Stars of purple, blue, silver, and green swirled around our fingers, roiling in black shadows as my own magic rose from within. Singing in my blood, my magic flooded every pore, yearning to combine with his.

A rush surged through me, and the tiny cosmos between our hands exploded into a million pieces above our heads. No longer were we in a throne room in Egypt but joined together, entwined, and dancing as spirits among the stars. My heart raced, every nerve electrified. Energy pulsed around me, strengthening me and bringing me to life. This was true power, and now it was a part of me.

"Milly, open your eyes." Roarke's deep voice was smooth and calm and seemed to have even more of an effect on me now.

I opened my eyes and smiled, my body urging to be closer to his. We were back in the ancient throne room, and he was dressed again in his black cloak. And now I had one to match.

"It's official. You are my chosen queen." He released one hand, spinning me with the other.

I twirled, laughing and, for the first time in my life, feeling as if I truly belonged.

Walking up the corridor, we emerged from beneath the sphinx, its hidden passage secret again as we reset the Dream Stele in place.

"Now what?" I asked, not sure if I should be doing something or what came next.

"Now whenever you fall asleep, you'll immediately join me here, and our magic will work together to create balance throughout the world."

I smiled. "You've said that before, but what exactly does it mean?"

"If you're asking whether you have specific tasks to do, then the answer is no. Your presence and our combined magic is all that's required. We can simply continue exploring the dreamscape together, and the rest will happen automatically."

Thunder clapped in the distance, yanking my attention to the darkening sky. Lightning-streaked clouds formed on the horizon, churning and swelling with much-needed rain.

"That seems strange. I thought it almost never rained here."

Roarke took my hand, and in an instant, we were standing atop the largest of the three pyramids, fully surrounded by the building storm. "Giza usually receives less than one inch of rainfall per year, yet here we are, standing atop a natural wonder and witnessing another. It's this type of balance our magic creates."

My eyes snapped to his. "Are you saying this is happening in the real world as well?"

Roarke dipped his head, and I wavered on my feet.

I could see why it was dangerous for only one person to hold this much power. And still, I didn't know if the two of us would be enough. I stared out over the desert, flushed with pride that he'd chosen me.

"Thank you for choosing me to be your partner. Your... *queen.* I'm truly honored and only hope my magic is powerful enough to bring you the balance you need."

Roarke turned to me, placing a hand on either side of my face. "Milly, you're the most powerful witch I've ever encountered, and I don't even think you know it."

I followed his eyes as they dipped to my lips, my breath catching as he leaned in. His kiss was soft, gentle, and reminded me of the first time I dreamt of kissing him back in my room. Embarrassed, I pulled back.

"I'm sorry. Is this not okay?" he asked.

"No. I mean, yes, it is. I just feel silly. When I first met you, I thought you'd shown up in my room for real, and I imagined kissing you just like this."

Roarke's eyes darkened, a sensual smile spreading across his lips. "You didn't imagine it, Milly. I was there."

My mouth dropped open, heat flushing my face.

Roarke's infectious laugh spilled into the sky. "Milly, I've waited for you for so long, hoping and praying one day you'd see me in your dreams. By the time you kissed me, I was already in love with you." He took both my hands in his. "We are meant to be."

In love with me? I stared into his sparkling eyes, my heart racing as a crash of thunder sounded in the distance. Energy crackled between us, sparking a deep desire in me like I'd never felt before.

With a wave of my hand, I returned us to his forest.

Strong arms encircled my waist, lifting me off the ground. He walked us back into the house, not missing a step. My hands found purchase in his thick dark hair as I deepened our kiss.

I was done being scared. Over the years, I'd battled all kinds of uncertainty alone, so why should this be any different? I would face my fears head on, and if that led me straight into heartbreak, so be it.

Roarke moaned against my lips, the vibration traveling along my bones as he guided us deeper into the cabin and straight to his bed.

"Are you sure about this?" Roarke stared into my eyes, his firing silver and sparking my desire to even greater heights.

"I am. I want you, Roarke. And all of this." I tossed back my head, bringing my dream to life. The ceiling above us exploded, and it was once again night. With the sky our only backdrop, I pulled Roarke toward the bed and lay down upon it.

It was bold, but I welcomed him between my legs.

Supporting himself with a hand on either side of my head, Roarke trailed featherlight kisses down my neck until he reached the top of my breasts. "I won't go any farther without your permission."

I smiled up at him and winked, removing the top part of our clothing with just a thought.

Roarke glanced down, a sensual smile overtaking his lips before resuming their path along my skin.

I'd dreamed of this for so long, wondering what it would be like to make love with someone who loved me back.

Dropping an elbow, Roarke rolled us over, perching me on top of him. I sat up, unabashed, with my hands resting against his chest. He grabbed my hips, his fingers digging in as he slightly pushed up beneath me.

"Milly, I'm going to ask you again. Are you sure about this?"

I nodded. There was nothing left of my doubts and fears but charred remains, burned to ashes by my flaming desire. "Roarke," I whispered his name as his hands glided across my skin.

His touch was slow and precise, stretching out every moment into a treasured memory. I'd imagined moments like this before, but never in a million years had I pictured this—the Weaver of dreams as my lover.

He rolled us over again, and I peered up through my dark lashes, the image of his broad shoulders and the shape of him hovering over me scorched into my being. Whether he was truly in love with me or not, I accepted the outcome because I could no longer deny that I was in love with him.

"Roarke." My voice came out huskier than usual as I met his gaze. His eyes twinkled, and a slow grin curled his lips. God, I loved that smile.

"Milly," he whispered my name on a ragged breath and dropped his head to my bare skin.

Silver sparks flared around us, casting us in a familiar glow. We were back in the heavens again—body, mind, and soul.

I closed my eyes and let go. Waves of passion radiated from our bodies, flowing into the cosmos and disrupting the stars.

"Breathe, Milly. Nothing bad can happen to us here." Without words, he'd sensed my thoughts, and for once I was grateful.

I peered up into his eyes, my fingers playing in the wisps of his hair. "I've never been afraid to be alone before, but now I think you've ruined me."

"I'm the one who is ruined," he breathed out on a whisper, revealing his hidden truth. "For over a hundred years, I've fulfilled my duty, yet all I want to do now is drift through the universe, lost in your embrace."

I tossed back my head, gone at his words, and offered myself to him. A wave of desire engulfed me as we became one, and like magic, everything else was forgotten. I pulled him down and drank in his kisses as though I'd been dying of thirst. Words fell away as our bodies sang, quivering with each thrust and wave of pleasure. Nearing release, tears formed in my eyes as the love I felt for Roarke finally broke free. Our bodies trembled, shaking the surrounding planets on their axes as we tumbled together back through the stars.

14

"ARE YOU OKAY?" ROARKE'S DEEP VOICE DRIFTED over me like a silk sheet. As he laid his hand across my bare stomach, I realized we were both still lying naked in his bed.

"I'm fine, but thank you for asking." My cheeks heated, embarrassment flooding back as I pulled the blankets up over us both.

Roarke slid his arm under my head and pulled me close, holding me against him as silence overtook the room. I could feel our hearts beating in our respective chests, listening as they synced as if becoming one.

"Do you regret what happened?" Roarke's voice was low and shaky. Tentative and uneasy. And it made my heart break.

I leaned up on my elbow, looking him straight in the eyes. "Of course not. I may doubt my role in all this, but I don't doubt my feelings for you."

His face relaxed. "Good, because I love you, Milly, and that's something you should never doubt."

I love you, Milly. Finally… the words my soul longed to hear.

I felt myself opening up, truly believing we were written in the stars. From the first moment I noticed him in my dreams, I knew he was the man I wanted. And he was right. We were meant to be together. Forever.

I sat up, my nakedness no longer uncomfortable. "Is there some sort of ceremony we should have to solidify our commitment to one another?" I pictured a rose-lined aisle leading to the glass greenhouse on the grounds of Windsor Castle.

"Beyond what happened when we combined our magic?"

I tilted my head. "I hadn't realized that was a ceremony."

He sat up, scooting to rest his back against the headboard. "It might not have included chants or rituals or had any witnesses to confirm what we did, but there's nothing more sacred than combining our magic and you accepting your role as my queen. No one can separate us unless it's a decision we make for ourselves."

His words hit me differently, like a cold splash of water against scorched skin. He could choose to separate us if he wanted? Leaving me for a different queen?

I shimmied out of bed. "I suppose I should get back and let you get some rest."

He laughed but let me go. "It's not like the world ever really sleeps. You could stay here all day if you wanted. There's always work to be done."

I dressed in a hurry, my thoughts rolling over his words. "Does that mean our magic is working together in the dreamscape even when I'm not here?" Again, one more thing I didn't understand.

"Yes. That's the beauty of it. As a mortal witch, you can still live your life while our magic makes a difference here."

"But you're mortal too, aren't you? You said yourself that this home exists in the real world."

"Yes, this home and I are real, but because of my magic, we have to remain hidden. So it's just easier for me to spend most of my time here."

Easier or less lonely? I thought.

"I know you said we can't be together in the real world, but I still don't understand why."

"I'm sorry for sounding like a broken record, but it simply boils down to the rules. Weavers cannot interact for long periods of time in the real world without causing a disruption to our magic here." He rose from the bed and with a swipe of his hand was dressed again.

"All you need to do is live your life as you always have during the day, then join me here when you're ready to sleep at night. It's a perfect balance. But if you want to spend more time with me"—he winked—"like I said, there's always work to be done."

I laughed, leaning up to place a kiss on his lips. "Yes, well, I might pop in now and again, but my home still requires attention during the day. So will you see me out?"

Roarke scooped me into his arms, lifting me off my feet and walking us out the front door. Setting me down on the frost-covered path, he returned my simple kiss with a deep, passionate one of his own. "I'll be waiting for your return tonight, my love. See you then."

A rip opened up, and I walked through, waking on my couch as I emerged from a deep, satisfying sleep.

My love. Two more words I never thought I'd hear.

"Milly, one day you'll find a man who pulls at your very soul. Everything inside you will feel like it's falling apart but at the same time clicking together like the missing pieces of a puzzle. Only then will you know your heart has made its choice."

"Is that what you felt with Daddy?"

"That and more. Your father and I knew the instant we met that we'd be together forever." Mama lowered her head, plucking another pea pod from its stalk. *"But old wounds and the stretch of time had other plans."*

Pulling a bag of peas from the freezer, I recalled Mama's words. My father passed when I was so young, but thanks to her memories and all the stories she told, I'd always felt close to him regardless of his absence.

Stirring the ham hock in the bottom of my deep pot, I poured the tiny green seeds into the boiling water. It was an addition Mama made on the fly, adding an extra layer of flavor to her famous ham and white bean soup. Jenks purred at my feet while I continued to monitor and stir the stock.

"I wish you could meet Roarke, sweet boy. But I don't think that will ever be possible."

Jenks yowled, and I shared his frustration. It was going to be difficult to have a relationship I couldn't share with anyone. Not that I had anyone who cared, except Keelyn of course, but still… it would have been nice if the two of them could have met.

By midday, the smells wafting from the kitchen had my stomach growling while the pull in my chest had me longing to return to Roarke. He said I could enter the dreamscape anytime, not having to wait until I fell asleep at night. I contemplated the thought as I ladled a helping of the hearty broth into my bowl and prepared a small dish for Jenks as well. Setting it on the floor by his regular food, I returned to my worn wooden farm table with a glass of water and dug in. Mama and I had shared so many meals here. At times it was as if I could almost see her sitting across from me still.

"Mama, I met someone, and I'm finally in love," I spoke to her empty chair. "We are meant to be, and he loves me too." The words felt childish coming off my tongue, but the smile they elicited was completely genuine.

"The magic we create together can do great things for the world." I took a sip of my soup. "I think you would be proud."

The fire in the hearth flared, sending angry sparks crackling into the air and spilling onto the floor. I rushed to retrieve the metal tongs and pushed the offending log back into place, stomping the embers. Returning to the kitchen, I reclaimed my seat and took another spoonful of soup, keeping my eyes on the flames. Smoke wafted from the chimney, causing Jenks to yowl. But just like before, I couldn't see anything within the dark coils of fog that should be upsetting him.

Just then a knock on my door startled us both, and I jumped to my feet. "Who's there?"

"It's just me, Keelyn."

I opened the door and welcomed my friend inside.

"Sorry to just drop by, but since you refuse to get a phone, I didn't have a choice," she teased, her smile brightening the room. "Anyway, I just wanted to tell you that we're bumping up the book club to tonight if you still wanted to stop by."

I didn't, but I'd already said yes, so it would be impolite to back out now. "Okay. Sure. Thanks for letting me know."

"Also, I wanted to give you this…"

I glanced down at the bundle in her hands and quickly invited her in. "Have you had lunch yet?" I walked to the kitchen, trying not to seem too eager about the book in her hands.

"No, not yet, and I'm not going to lie. Whatever you have on the stove smells delicious."

I laughed and gestured for her to take a seat at the table while I dished her up a bowl of soup. "Why are you having to move the book club this week?" I asked, struggling as usual with the simple task of small talk.

Keelyn took a sip from the cup of water I'd placed beside her plate. "One of the ladies who actually *did* like the book has to leave town tomorrow and wanted to make sure her thoughts would be heard." She shook her head. "Who knew a book club could be so dramatic?"

I set the bowl of soup in front of her, cringing at the thought of being in attendance tonight.

"But that's kind of the point, isn't it?" Keelyn went on. "I love hearing how each reader gets something different out of the story. You know what they say... No two readers ever read the same book."

I grinned, not really understanding her meaning as my eyes darted to the book lying on the table beside her. It was somewhat small and unassuming with a plain black jacket and gold lettering embossed on the cover.

"So... are you going to tell me what that's about?" I lifted my chin.

"Of course." She picked up the book and handed it to me. "After the last time we talked, I went back to the library and input the search for any dream books that mentioned the word weaver, and when I went in this morning, I had a hit."

I glanced down at the title, taking in the slightly raised and blocky font on the front.

The Queen of Nightmares

That sounded ominous.

"Turns out we actually had a copy already."

"Really? I swear I've been over that entire section many times."

"Yes, well, it wasn't in the nonfiction or metaphysical area. It was filed in the fiction section instead."

"Fiction?" I raised a brow, turning the book over in my hands.

"Yep. I think it's the only fictional book Genevieve DuWant ever wrote."

The snap of wood popping in the hearth filled my ears, muffling any other sound in the room. This book was written by the same author as the other book I'd been drawn to. Obviously, there was something there I had missed.

"Milly… are you okay?" Keelyn stood, placing a hand on my shoulder and guiding me back down into my chair. "You look like you got dizzy all of a sudden."

"Yes. Sorry. I'm fine." I laid the book back on the table and swallowed a few gulps of water.

My mind raced over the details I remembered from the other book, snagging on one in particular.

While I cannot prove what I say is true, I can document my experiences and share them here as a warning—

Opening the book, I flipped it from front to back, inspecting the jacket cover and reading the author's note printed on the inside sleeve.

While the words I share here are true, this book has been published as fiction so that I may maintain the secrecy of my source. For if I were to disclose their existence, the world would never be the same.

My world shifted.

"Milly, what is it?" Keelyn's voice snapped me back to the table.

"Um…" I blinked. "It says here that while this book is fiction, the contents are true. I guess I just don't understand how that's accurate or possible." I shook my head and set the book down.

"Hmm, that's interesting. I've only ever seen one other book like that before. It was so the author could protect her sources."

"That's what this one says too, but what does it mean?" I slurped another bite from my spoon, my soup now bordering on cold.

"As you know, in nonfiction books, the bibliography is where the author has to list all of her sources and document any research material used for the book. *But…* if the author is unwilling to share that information, they can choose to publish their work as fiction instead." She shrugged. "Then it's up to the reader to decide whether they believe them or not."

"Wow. I've never heard of that," I admitted. "What was the other book?"

"*The Expected One* by Kathleen McGowan. It was a religious text… and an amazing story."

"I'll have to check it out." My eyes drifted to the book in front of me, knowing I wouldn't be reading anything else.

15

KEELYN AND I FINISHED LUNCH WITH A flurry of conversation ranging from books to gardening tips back to books and of course eventually landing on guys.

"Have you seen Thomas lately?" Keelyn asked with a raised brow. "I may be quite a few years older than him, but I'm not dead. He's looking *pretty* good." She laughed.

I blushed and shook my head, trying my best to ignore the book still resting on the table.

Thomas Kendrix was another boy who grew up here and was now ready to make his way in the world as a man at the ripe age of twenty-six. He *was* gorgeous, and I had definitely noticed on my last trip to his parents' bakery, but that didn't matter now.

"Yes, he certainly is. But I think he and Rachel are a thing."

"Really?" She gasped.

"Last time I went in, the two of them were huddled in the corner while his mom took my order."

"All right. Well, good for them!" Keelyn grinned and raised her cup, toasting the new couple that would no doubt be the talk of the town by the end of the day. "Speaking of... do you have your eye on anyone yet?"

I tilted my head, Roarke's face filling my mind's eye. "No." I lied. "You know me... I'm good on my own. How about you?" If she was going to pry, then so would I. Friends were allowed to do that, right?

"Nah. After my divorce, I found that friends, family, and the occasional fling were enough for me." She raised her glass of water again. "Cheers to being an independent woman."

I lifted mine as well, Roarke's words floating through my mind. *Deep down, I think you are lonely.*

The image of his broad shoulders hovering over me formed in my mind's eye, and a smile burst onto my face.

Not anymore, I thought.

"What are you grinning at?" Keelyn teased.

"Nothing. I'm just... happy, I guess."

Her brows rose into her hairline. "Milly Atwood, happy? Wow. I never thought I'd see the day," she teased.

"What? Are you saying I'm some miserable teenage girl who only mopes around the library when she wants to talk to her only friend?" I made fun of myself, knowing that was exactly what I was.

I preferred my solitude, and if that meant projecting a certain *vibe*, I was happy to do it. It kept me safe, and now that I had Roarke, I'd be spending even less time in town. So all in all, I thought my ruse was working pretty well. No one needed to know how satisfied I was, living my magical life alone in the woods.

Memories of running through the forest with Mama slammed into me. The joy and freedom we'd cultivated here pulsed deep within our land, and I couldn't be prouder. Even if no one else ever understood.

"Well, it's true. Do you mind if I cancel on book club tonight? Because nothing would make me happier than sitting by this fire, reading the book you found for me." I stood and retrieved it from the kitchen table. "Honestly, I can't thank you enough."

Keelyn hugged me goodbye, smiling wide. "I figured as much. And you're completely welcome. I hope it helps you find what you're looking for."

Me too, I thought as I showed her to the door.

I looked at the clock, noting I only had a few hours left before nightfall. I needed to read as much of this book as I could because if it revealed even the smallest detail or any new information about the Weaver and his magic, I wanted to know it before I returned to the dreamscape tonight.

Leaving the book on the cushions, I stoked the fire and refilled my cup, then planted myself back on the couch with my feet tucked beneath Jenks's warm fur.

"Okay, buddy, here we go."

Cracking the spine, I skipped the introduction and flipped straight to chapter one.

Our whole lives, we've been led to believe our dreams are the work of our subconscious. But I'm here to tell you that is not entirely true.

From the first sentence, I was hooked. Now four hours later and after reading a quarter of the book, I was happy to find out the Weaver was telling the truth. He was the manipulator of a special kind of magic and responsible for influencing the dreams of us all.

I set down the book and headed for the shower. I needed to get ready for bed so I could return to the dreamscape and tell Roarke what I found.

As I lathered my hair, the shampoo's vanilla scent drifted to my nose, easing my frazzled nerves. I wasn't nervous about seeing Roarke again after what had happened between us. Actually, I was excited to return to his arms. But what I did question was his reaction to this book. I wondered if he knew it existed at all, and the more I thought about it, the less I felt like sharing the news. Something that revealed his magic to the world seemed wrong, and I suddenly felt guilty for reading it in the first place. If I told him about it now, it would only prove I still hadn't trusted him even when I said I did.

Finished, I wrapped myself in a towel and returned to where I left the book sitting on the side table next to the couch. Its size reminded me of a Bible like the kind you'd find in hotel drawers or the backs of your local church pews. But the secrets carried within were enormous and something I didn't want out in the world.

I thought about what Keelyn might say when I told her I wasn't returning the book. I'd purchase it from the library, of course, but how would she react when I asked her not to replace it?

Maybe I *should* tell Roarke about it after all. Then we could search out any other copies and destroy them together. I shook my head. The idea seemed ridiculous and dramatic and went against everything in my bones, but I couldn't deny the protective urge surging inside me. The Weaver's world and magic were ours alone.

Slipping into my flannel nightgown, I returned to the kitchen for another cup of tea. I still wasn't sure what to do as I settled beneath the afghan on the couch, not quite ready to go to sleep. But by the time I took my last sip, my eyelids were drooping closed, pulling me farther down into the cushions and immediately into the dreamscape again.

"Hi there. Is everything okay?" Roarke's voice was hesitant, wary. I opened my eyes and found us back in his hidden forest.

"Everything's fine. I just had some things to do before I could go to sleep." The lie coated my tongue, its presence viscous and sticky inside my mouth.

"Well, I'm glad you're finally here." He stepped up beside me and took my hand, the leaves and sticks snapping beneath his boots as he pulled us forward. "I've got something I want to show you."

Walking in the opposite direction of the cabin, we emerged at a place within the forest I'd never seen before. Water stretched on forever, seeming to surround us, revealing even more of the hidden truth about where he actually lived.

"I didn't correct you when you thought I lived on a lake, but in reality, my cabin resides on a secluded island, hidden from everyone in the dreamscape *and* the real world." He turned to me, twirling a piece of hair that had fallen from my braid around his finger. "But I wanted you to know the truth."

Guilt ate further into my gut as I thought about the book. "Thank you for telling me. I know how special this place is to you, and I'm honored you're willing to share it with me."

He pulled me close.

"I've told you before that I want to share everything with you. That will never change."

I spun out of his embrace, feeling unworthy and sick to my stomach.

"Milly, are you sure you're okay? You seem... distraught." Roarke stepped up beside me.

I clenched my middle and sank to my knees. "I need to tell you something, and I'm not sure how you're going to react."

He bent down, sitting among the leaves, and gently eased his arm around me. "You can tell me absolutely anything."

16

THE WORDS DIED ON MY TONGUE, THE fear of revealing the secret too overwhelming to voice out loud. "Never mind. It's nothing."

Roarke's side-glance told me he wasn't buying it. "Are you sure? You seem pretty upset."

"I'm sure." I shrugged, playing it off. "I just saw another news report about something happening in one of the places we visited before. But you're right. It has nothing to do with us." I pushed to stand, kicking around the yellow and brown leaves with the tip of my boot, hating myself more and more by the minute.

"Is there somewhere we need to go tonight?" I asked, desperate for an escape.

Roarke gave me a pensive look—as though he still didn't believe me—but his eyes remained kind as they met mine. "You know the drill. All you have to do is pick a place."

I turned away, feeling a crevice opening inside me, and in the next instant, we were perched on the edge of the glorious Grand Canyon. "I've always wanted to see it with my own eyes."

"Great choice! It's one of my favorite modern wonders of the world."

The sun was just beginning to set, and the colors radiating from the canyon walls mimicked its power in a vibrant spectrum of oranges and reds.

I leaned forward, peering out over the edge. "It's enormous. Its size is hard to comprehend from pictures alone."

"Indeed. But do you want an even better view?"

I nodded without even knowing what he meant. In the next second, we were standing at the side of a beautiful waterfall and aqua-blue pool. The lush green trees and red rocks surrounding it created the most vivid and contrasting image. Its beauty was so overwhelming it brought tears to my eyes.

"Look up," Roarke instructed.

I did and almost wept.

The stunning oasis was at the bottom of the Grand Canyon, seemingly wedged between the cracks of two rock faces.

"This is Havasu Falls and probably one of the most famous Havasupai waterfalls on the reservation.

"What do you mean?"

"There are five Havasupai falls located within the Indian reservation, which is in an offshoot canyon next to the main one. Tourists can book reservations with the tribe to either hike or pack mule down to this site."

I turned back to this hidden gem, awed by the juxtaposition between the harsh desert surrounding it and the beautiful paradise before me. "I honestly have no words." Overwhelmed, I walked to the water's edge with tears trickling down my cheeks. "Can we get in?"

Roarke waved a hand in the air, filling the sky with shooting stars while a turquoise light glowed from beneath the water's depths. "Of course."

I met his eyes and was flooded with emotions I'd rarely felt before. Lust definitely, but there was something else... Gratefulness, perhaps? I wasn't sure, but as I walked into the warm water, I waved my own hand and removed my clothes.

Roarke followed me in, scooping me into his arms and kissing me softly. "I'm glad you like it."

"How could I not? It's incredible." I pulled back. "And so are you." I wrapped my legs around his middle and let my mind and body float away.

Roarke kissed me again, this time deeply. Passionately. And we spent the rest of our night locked in each other's arms, lost to the world around us.

By morning, we'd hiked the canyon, picnicked on the plateau above, and flown to the North Rim for a glass of wine at the lodge as we watched the sun set over the rim.

"This has been one of my favorite trips so far," I admitted, not caring I'd spent almost twenty-four hours in the dreamscape with him.

"Me too." Roarke reached behind his back, pulling out a cactus blossom in full bloom. "For your collection."

I took the flower, sniffing its sweet scent, then tucked it behind my ear. "Thank you." I thought about the viola still sitting on my altar at home. "But how is it I can bring something from the dreamscape back with me into the real world?"

Roarke shrugged. "Just another perk to my Weaver magic."

I lifted my glass to my lips, the sweet wine puckering the taste buds at the back of my mouth. I thought back to all the times he'd used that same excuse or deemed something "just part of the rules." But now, after seeing into his soul, it no longer felt like he was hiding something from me, but perhaps something was being hidden from him. What if there were aspects of his magic that even *he* didn't understand?

"You mean *our* Weaver magic now, right?" I smiled, shifting my train of thought.

"Yes. *Our* magic."

Plates of fish, salads, and steamed vegetables were brought to the table, served alongside a basket of freshly baked bread.

"Mmm... This smells delicious."

"Let's dig in." Roarke's eyes never left mine as he lifted a forkful of greens to his mouth, but a commotion outside the lodge pulled my attention away.

People in uniforms ran past the windows, heading to the edge of the rim

"What's happened?" I asked the waitress who had stopped in the middle of the room.

"Someone has fallen off the side of the canyon."

My eyes widened and met Roarke's again.

He shook his head. "As unfortunate as it is, this tends to happen now and again. The winds blowing up from the canyon are so strong they can knock a person right off the trail." He leaned closer across the table. "This has nothing to do with us."

My eyes tracked the medical personnel running back and forth outside, snagging solidly on the gurney and a body bag being carried toward the scene.

"I'd like to go home now." I dropped my fork, its tines clanging against my plate.

Roarke nodded and waved his hand, and the lodge disappeared.

"What are we doing back here?" I asked, looking out over the water of the Weaver's island.

"I want to make sure you're okay before I send you home alone." He moved to take my hand, his brow creased with worry, but I pulled away. "Milly, talk to me. Please."

I sat down on the cold bank, my feet barely escaping the water's grasp. "I understand that people have nightmares, but I have a horrible feeling that what just happened will be the first thing I see on the morning news." I looked up at him from beneath my dark lashes. "You said it yourself. Our magic is how things can happen in both places, so how is this any different?"

Roarke lowered himself onto the bank beside me. "It's different because I *will* those things to follow you home. But not this. Nightmares like this are just a part of life, and as Weavers, we can't escape being witnesses to it all."

I pulled my knees tightly to my chest. "Well, I don't like it."

"I know, Milly. And I'm sorry." The warmth of his arm settling around my shoulders was a welcome comfort. And in that moment, I realized how sheltered I'd truly been.

Mama had created a world where our simple way of life protected me, keeping me buffered from the harsh realities of existence. Sure, I'd witnessed death before—in nature with the wild animals that lived in our woods—but I'd never had to face it head on. The realization made me feel silly and insecure.

"I guess I never realized how much Mama protected me. But you're right. It is all just a part of life." I raised my chin, looking out over the water with a newfound sense of strength, and swore to stop burying my head in the sand. I might be naïve about some things, but I wasn't stupid, and things like this *did* happen every day all over the world. I just had to get used to having a front-row seat to it all.

I turned to Roarke. Worry lines pulled at the corners of his eyes, and he was looking at me as if he thought I might break.

"I'm fine. I swear. But I am ready to go home."

He leaned in and kissed my cheek. "See you tomorrow night?" His vulnerability was on full display now. Every move he made was tinged with fear or filled with worry he'd do something to upset me. And *that* broke my heart.

I woke with a start, back on the couch, my legs heavy and weak from sleeping all night and day.

Jenks's purr vibrated through the house, loud and angry.

"It's okay, boy. I'm here, and I'm fine." I slunk into the kitchen, filling his empty food bowl and pouring him some fresh milk. "I'm sorry, baby. That had to be scary for you." I rubbed a hand down his back, his small frame rising to meet my apologetic touch.

It was still dark out, but I wasn't tired. I pulled a jar of last year's marmalade from the fridge and grabbed a stack of crackers from the pantry.

Back on the couch, I flicked on the TV, happy the news wasn't yet blaring on the screen. I didn't watch many shows, usually occupying my hands with gardening or some other magical task, but tonight I only wanted to sit there and get lost in something that had nothing to do with the real world.

Switching between an infomercial on the greatest vacuum sealer ever made and the artistic stylings of a long-dead painter, I finally landed on a nature channel filled with calming trees and chirping birds. The sounds filled my small cottage with a much-needed sense of peace. It reminded me of our trip to the jungle, and I suddenly wondered if I could return without an escort now that I was officially his queen.

The last time I tried, I ended up right outside Roarke's cabin, but tonight I was determined to do this on my own.

With my snack left behind on the side table, I rushed to my altar and lit the smudge stick lying in my abalone shell.

God and Goddess, cleanse any negative energy from me so that I may only be filled with love and light.

I wafted the smoke up and down my body, making sure to encircle my head and feet. Grabbing a chunk of blue lace agate, I walked to my bed, excited and confident. I could do this. Lying down, I repeated my previous spell while picturing the jungle in my mind's eye.

Goddess of night, hear my plea. Shroud me from the one who sees. Let me walk within my dreams, shielded and alone. So mote it be.

Cool water lapped at my toes, and I woke to the glowing colors of the jungle again. The waterfall rained down just as before, creating a mesmerizing light show as its force churned the surface of the pond.

I looked around, expecting to see Roarke appear, but so far, I was alone.

Smiling wide, I waded in, my one-piece swimsuit already back in place. Sinking up to my chin, I paddled out to the middle, then rolled over and floated on my back. Bright blue and yellow macaws flew overhead, their loud squawks penetrating my ears even below the waterline.

Tiny bubbles tickled my skin as I moved my arms back and forth. Trails of silver light shimmered all around my body—the Weaver's magic present in the dreamscape even when he wasn't around.

Closing my eyes, I let the cacophony of jungle sounds lull me back to my center. Floating weightlessly, I was reminded of all the summers Mama and I spent at the small river that cut through the woods behind our house. In places, it was deep enough I could lift my feet, and together we'd spent hours drifting along with the current.

"Milly, whenever you find yourself lost, just return to the water. Its properties can heal even the deepest scars."

At the time, I didn't understand what she meant, but now I knew she was talking about my heart.

17

I FLOATED PEACEFULLY ALONE FOR THE NEXT hour before being yanked from my reverie by a powerful boom. Scrambling from the pond, I stood at the edge of the water and scanned the surrounding jungle.

High above the trees in the distance, smoke rose into the air in thick, choking plumes, turning the sky an ominous dark gray.

I squeezed the blue stone still in my palm and woke up safe and sound back in my own bed.

Once again, some sort of catastrophe had penetrated my dreams. And I didn't care what Roarke said… It was starting to feel like there was more to it than he was letting on.

Dawn finally broke in the real world, and I flipped on the TV, nestling under the blanket and intent on watching every story that flashed across the screen.

After a few commercial breaks, the reporter reappeared. "And in other news, three tourists were pulled from the North Rim of the Grand Canyon yesterday after a gust of up to sixty-five miles per hour blew them from the trail, ending their lives.

I gasped. *There were three?*

Clutching the blanket to my chest, I waited for the next report. A knot formed in my throat as images of the Amazon rainforest appeared, along with huge swaths of barren land and burning trees.

"Protests continue in the jungles of South America as developers threaten the region with a massive construction push that's leading to unimaginable deforestation," the lady reported.

Tears burned my eyes as I stared at alternating images of birds and all manner of wildlife scrambling to survive as their habitats were torn to shreds, floods raging where trees no longer stood in their way, the soil eroding into dangerous crevices as the water rushed toward a village below, and trucks and trailers filled with logs mutilating the ground as they rolled through the jungle on their unforgiving, oversized tires.

I was heartbroken, thinking back to the beautiful place in my dream, and I didn't understand why the Weaver couldn't do anything about it. Why *we* couldn't do anything about it.

I pushed from the couch, desperate to put my anger to good use.

Grabbing a bundle of lavender from the rafters in the back room, I stomped to my altar and lit the white candle already standing at attention in its golden base.

Goddess of all, hear my plea. Sprinkle peace onto the world I see. Calm and soothe the hearts of man, bringing balance back to the land.

I crushed the lavender between my palms, letting the petals float down into the candle's flame. Sparks popped and snapped as the dried flowers burned, releasing the magic of my rushed spell.

I wasn't sure if what I'd done would help in the grand scheme of things, but I couldn't just sit here and do nothing. I at least had to try to help.

I left the candle burning as I reclaimed my seat on the couch, waiting to see the next set of reports as they came around. Within the next half hour, an update filled the screen, and I cheered internally. Barricades had been erected at the site of the commercial loggers in South America, halting further progress while new negotiations took place.

Whether it had anything to do with me, I wasn't sure. But it certainly felt good nonetheless.

Sunlight filtered through the double-pane windows at the front of the house, brightening the cottage and lifting my mood even further. I snatched Jenks up into my arms and spun around.

"What shall we do today, Mr. Jenkins? Hike through the woods, looking for mice? Venture to town and purchase a new apron? Or perhaps..." I let Jenks jump out of my arms as I went to look for the little black book I'd left in the other room. "We could run to the library and return this to Keelyn after all."

A slight shock zapped my fingers, and I jerked back, dropping the book to the floor. Its spine hit hard and spilled open, revealing a drawing sprawled across the pages within.

I bent down and retrieved the book, inspecting the charcoal outline of a witch standing over a bubbling cauldron, and read the caption below it.

Agitha, the disgruntled witch who cursed a Weaver
when she *wasn't* chosen to be his queen.

"What in the world?" My knees gave out, and I dropped back
onto the couch, crossing my legs and reading on.

Cursed to exist alone in the real world, the Weaver
line has struggled to reproduce while being bound in
the dreamscape ever since.

Struggled but succeeded, I thought as I stared at the tiny tome,
realizing it had more secrets to share. If this were true, then it was
why Roarke and I couldn't be together in the real world. He'd said
it was because of the "rules," and I assumed he would have told me
about a curse. Unless…

I walked back to my altar, marking my place in the small black
book with the sprig of flowers that was left after my spell. Gripping
the book tightly in hand, I grabbed my pendulum from the small
drawer of the wooden box I kept it in. Positioning the hanging point
of the rose quartz over the book, I focused my intent and asked my
question.

*Lord and Lady, guide my talisman with your highest light and tell me the
truth. Does the Weaver know about his curse?*

I felt the pendulum move in my hand and opened my eyes. It
was swinging in the *no* direction, confirming my fears.

I shook my head. "My god, he doesn't know."

How was I supposed to tell an all-powerful being that his entire family line had been cursed?

I shuffled back to the living room, my feet dragging across the hardwood floor as I thought about the implications. Obviously, he needed a female to further the Weaver line, but whether that was all this was, I was no longer sure. Was the balance he spoke of regarding his queen related to having children as well? I thought I was chosen because of my magic alone. Because we were meant to be. God, I was tired of feeling stupid.

I flopped down on my bed, burying my face in my pillow. The idea of Roarke using me—unknowingly or not—sickened me. But it wasn't all his fault. I had chosen this. Accepted him and his magic into my life. I wanted it and was happy with how things were going between us. But now everything just felt like a lie.

I sobbed into the down pillow, saturating the cotton cover with my angry tears. The more I thought about it, the more my stomach roiled in warning, telling me I'd need to keep this to myself. But how? How could I return to the dreamscape and act like nothing was wrong? Or perhaps I didn't have to.

An idea formed, and I rolled over, cocking my arm over my eyes. If I created an elixir that kept me up all night, I could finish reading the book and gather the information I'd need to deal with this on my own.

The idea knotted in my chest, and I let myself cry, releasing a flood of doubts and fears until I had no more to shed. Sunlight beamed through the front windows, betraying the cool temperature outside as it lit up my cottage in the early morning hours. I'd have plenty of time to work on my elixir later and wondered if I took a nap now, could I do so without entering my dreams? I was emotionally exhausted and yearned for an escape.

My idea had merit, but I'd need to think this through. If I could find the witch, or any of her remaining line, I could break the curse. Then Roarke and I could be together in the real world and nothing else would matter.

I called Jenks to my side. "I'm going to take a quick nap, but I need you to connect to me and keep me grounded here."

Jenks nuzzled under my extended hand, flipping it up and onto his back. And with my familiar in place, I closed my eyes again.

18

By MIDMORNING, I WOKE REENERGIZED AND ready to start making my plans. I hadn't seen Roarke or visited any vibrant dreamscapes while I slept, thanks to Jenks and the remnants of the spell I'd cast earlier to wander alone. Now I needed to prepare my elixir and finish reading this book. If what it revealed so far was any indication of the knowledge held within, I couldn't wait to learn more. But first, breakfast.

Cracking two eggs into the cast-iron skillet, I added pepper, salt, and a dash of cayenne and started to stir. I liked my eggs a little spicy, scrambled, and with a bit of turkey and mushroom. And so did Jenks. Sitting patiently at my feet, he waited for me to scoop a helping into his bowl.

"Here you go, sweetie. Thanks again for standing guard over me while I napped."

He dug in without even a peep.

I returned to the couch, planning to read while I ate, but had forgotten my tea. The peppermint and ginseng blend would keep me focused and energized, which was exactly what I needed.

With my cup in hand, I turned back to the living room, my eyes catching on something beneath the white armchair that separated the space. Kneeling down, I reached under the front edge and pulled out the cactus flower Roarke had gifted me the night before. I *had* returned with it, but it must have dropped out of my hair when I woke up on the couch.

The velvet petals were still soft under my thumb. I thought about the viola hidden in the wooden box on my altar and went to retrieve it. Roarke had willed these two flowers through the veil of the dreamscape to remind me of our time together, and perhaps they could serve an even bigger purpose.

Grabbing a gold craft ring and spool of twine from the old wooden cabinet in my back room, I returned to the couch with the supplies in hand. Knotting the first strand, I pulled the twine back and forth between each side of the metal hoop, weaving a grid across the open space. Then, I weaved my mementos into the strands, pushing their stems through the "fence" of twine. He'd sent me home with something from each of our adventures, and while this wasn't exactly a dream catcher in the traditional sense, it was similar enough. It was a memory circle, and I'd use it to track my dreams. I never wanted to forget the things that happened, good or bad. It was simple, beautiful, and would hang perfectly above my bed, reminding me of my role in all of this.

With the tap of a nail, I hung it in place and returned to my breakfast, now unappealing and cold. Picking up the book instead, I flipped to the page where I'd stopped reading, disappointed in myself for not finishing in the first place. I'd almost discarded the most important piece of research I'd found on the Weaver, thinking there couldn't possibly be anything between the pages I didn't already know. Obviously, with a drop of the book, I was proven wrong and now found myself nervous to learn what else I might find. And I was right to worry.

The farther I read, the more upset I became. Genevieve DuWant clearly had a peek into the Weavers' world, cataloging their existence and magic all while keeping their title and names completely obscured. But it was her mention of the Queen of Nightmares that brought me to my knees. According to her source, Weavers used their queen's magic to twist the dreams of others, the *balance* they provide producing nightmares instead of peaceful dreams. And even worse, the only way to stop it was for their queen to walk away and relinquish her magic.

I tossed the book down. Was this what Roarke was doing as well? Slowly twisting my magic dark? I paced my living room, fuming and scared.

The fire in Tuscany, the accident in the Grand Canyon, the devastation happening in the jungle. I had no idea what I was going to do or how I could confront Roarke with any of this. It all seemed so far off from what Roarke's magic was about. From what *we* were about.

No. I couldn't believe he'd do this to me. And even if he was… I would *never* relinquish my magic to anyone.

Not even him.

I stifled another yawn, fighting the urge to close my eyes as the sun completed its descent for the day. Peels of orange and lime lay ready in my mortar, along with sprigs of peppermint, rosemary, and basil waiting to be ground into dust for my "stay awake" elixir. Mixed into my green tea and combined with my spell, it should keep me awake and out of the dreamscape entirely, at least for tonight. I needed more time to think, finish this book, and possibly alter my plans.

Perhaps if I could contact any of Ms. DuWant's children, they might be able to identify her source, which I desperately needed to do. Whether it was a previous Weaver or perhaps a queen who walked away, I needed to speak to them. To understand if what happened was a choice of that particular Weaver or if it was part of the curse as well.

I couldn't wrap my mind around Roarke knowingly hurting people, but I couldn't deny I'd barely scraped the tip of the magic in his world. Yet I'd agreed. At least from the sound of things, I still had a choice and could simply walk away if I had to.

My heart clenched in my chest. I couldn't think about this right now. The idea of leaving Roarke made me sick to my stomach. We'd just found one another. Declared our love. And as a girl who spent most of her life alone, I wasn't about to throw that away without obtaining solid facts. He was no longer a figment of my imagination. He was real, and I'd fight to discover the truth… for us both.

I pressed my pestle against the herbs and zest, grinding them together with a swirl of my wrist. I needed to make enough for a few pots of tea in case I didn't get as far as I needed within the next couple of days. I'd have to visit the library tomorrow to use the computers and search for Ms. DuWant's kids. Even then, it sounded like an impossible task since I was sure she'd used a pseudonym for all her books. It was either that or start tracking Agitha's origins and hope that led me somewhere instead.

The kettle whistled as my eyes dipped again. Scooping the spell powder into a cup, I poured the hot water over it and inhaled its energizing scent.

Mother of Night, hear my plea. Relinquish your hold and let me be. Awake to read and learn and grow. Grant me your energy, to and fro.

I took a sip of the tea and tossed back my head. A surge of power flowed through me, firing along each of my nerves and veins. Refocused and ready to work through the night, my mind veered toward Roarke again. What would he think when I didn't appear in the dreamscape tonight? Would he be mad? Worried? Or simply appear in my bedroom as he had before?

Panicked at the thought, I grabbed my sage and resmudged the crystal grid around my house for added protection, adding a sprig of juniper over each door and retracing all my apotropaic marks in the wood to strengthen my wards.

I had work to do, and I needed to focus, so if the Weaver wanted to visit me tonight, he'd have to break down the goddamn door.

19

By THREE A.M. I'D FINISHED THE BOOK, made my notes, and poured myself another cup of tea. With my clothes for my trip to the library laid out, I'd be ready and waiting when its doors opened in five short hours.

Keelyn would be surprised to see me, especially on the weekend, but I needed to pay for this book since I was definitely not returning it now. Plus, I knew my search for Genevieve DuWant's real name would most likely take all day.

Jenks was curled up on the rug in front of the fire, and I envied him. While my mind wasn't tired due to the spell, my body certainly could use the rest. A tightness lay across my shoulders, working its way up into my neck. I took another sip of tea, walking to the back room to find my pain-relieving cream.

Jars, vials, tubes, and tubs lined the cupboards and shelves, all products created by my own hand with ingredients grown on my land. There was a sense of pride that overtook me whenever I thought about it. Using all Mama had taught me, I truly had thrived on my own.

"I've witnessed a lot of young people lose their families, Milly, but I don't

believe any of them remained as strong as you." Roarke's words drifted through my mind, and the anxiety of him knowing so much more about me than I did of him overwhelmed me again.

From what he'd said, he hadn't been watching me as I initially thought, but I still got the sense that he knew more than he was letting on.

I rolled my neck and rubbed in the cayenne cream, my shoulders easing slowly but surely.

With a few more hours to wait, I filled my tub with hot water and stepped in. Steam rose from the surface, enveloping me in a hazy cloud. My shoulders stung as they sank below the water, the heat causing the cream to penetrate even deeper. Lying back against the cool porcelain, I closed my eyes and relaxed, thankful for the little slice of heaven Mama and I had created here.

Our home was a small, one-story cottage clapped in dark siding with varied peaks topping the roof. The copper shingles were aged and worn, settling into a dark green patina that allowed it to blend into the surrounding forest. Boxes, troughs, and various trellises filled the side yard, full of flowers, herbs, and edible plants, while a small shed in the back corner housed all my rakes, shovels, and larger equipment. I inhaled deeply, appreciating the aroma of the eucalyptus hanging from the bathroom door, and thought about the last time I'd worked the garden with Mama by my side.

"Be gentle, Milly, for if you tend the land with care, it will always take care of you in return."

She'd been right. About that and so much more. And in

[149]

moments like these, I missed her dearly.

A tear rolled down my cheek, sizzling as it met the hot water. I didn't cry much anymore, but I'd never deny my heart a release. Tears were the soul's way of telling our hidden story. Whether happy or sad, our emotions could be read within every drop. The story currently gliding down my face was one of loss, heartache, betrayal, and fear. I rested a hand over my chest, struggling to calm my racing heart. I'd have to weed through the tangled web inside my mind before returning to the dreamscape.

I washed, rinsed, and stepped from the tub, my sad story disappearing down the drain with a pull of the plug.

Rarely was I at odds with myself, but ever since Roarke entered my life, the push and pull inside me never seem to cease. I needed answers, definitive ones, and I wouldn't be sleeping until I found some today.

Dressed and with only an hour and a half left to wait, I remade my eggs from earlier and finally ate breakfast. Jenks rose from his spot near the fire, meandering closer, only to flop down at my feet.

"Well, aren't you just a ball of energy this morning?" I teased as he stretched his back, looking exactly like every black cat ever drawn for Halloween. Leaning down, I scratched behind his ears.

With my eyes lowered, I caught movement just beyond the front window and froze. There were no storms tonight or wind to blow the trees, so whatever was there was an unwelcome visitor.

Easing off the couch, I strode to the front door, gripping the machete I kept hidden beneath the bench. Yanking the door open,

I raised the knife overhead, ready to defend myself and Jenks. No one could hurt us here.

My vision swam in the deep shadows that hugged the corner of the house. But other than an adorable raccoon lumbering back into the woods, I didn't see anything out of place.

With my nerves firing on high alert, I scanned the trees, my eyes quickly adjusting to the dark. No one was there, but I couldn't stay put any longer. Rushing inside, I poured a thermos full of tea, then grabbed my coat and bag, shoving the book and sheathed machete inside. I'd be extremely early for my visit to the library, but there were plenty of other things I could do in the dark.

Gangly limbs of silhouetted trees lined the night sky, the moon as their backdrop piercing the veil. Silence reigned as most of the forest creatures had found their fill and turned in for the night. The soft glow of fireflies and lightning bugs guided my way down the leaf-laden path, drawing me deeper into the heart of the forest where the most glorious mysteries lay.

Coming to rest on a familiar stump, I pulled out my thermos and took a swig of my tea.

Then I waited.

The stars above held my attention, reminding me of Roarke, until a thick layer of clouds finally obscured the moon's face. The forest was thrust into its darkest self, and in retaliation, a new world burst to life.

Creatures and organisms began to glow all around me, their bioluminescence providing light in the darkest of times. I pulled the machete from my bag and scraped it against the trunk of a nearby oak, loosening the glowing lichen that grew along its base.

Mama taught me how to properly harvest the gifts the forest provides, using their special ingredients to create a magic of our own. Some of the phosphorescent organisms absorb light from the sun, giving it back later, while others actually produce light through a chemical reaction built into their DNA.

Regardless of the science, it was simply beautiful and never failed to take my breath away.

I continued gathering as many new ingredients as I could, already seeing the end results in my head. Creams, candles, and essential oils all infused with "fairy lights" would sell like wildfire at next season's market. Accompanied by my first crop of cosmos, baby's breath, and lavender ice tulips, the springtime tourists wouldn't be able to resist.

Satisfied with my magical trove, I headed back to the path that would take me to town. Keelyn was an early bird and should almost be to the library by now.

Emerging from the tree line, I spotted her car in its usual spot and ran up the stairs.

"Milly! What are you doing here so early? And on a Saturday no less."

"Hi, Keelyn. I have some important research I'll need a computer for, but also, I wanted to pay for this." I pulled the book out of my bag, keeping it pressed against my chest.

"I don't think it's overdue yet." She clicked at the keys of her computer, her brows creasing as she focused on the screen.

"No. It's not. But what I'm saying is… I need to buy this book."

Keelyn cocked her head, her quirky smile barely hiding what she thought of my odd request. "Are you sure you wouldn't rather just order a copy of your own?"

"I'm sure. I need to keep this one." Honestly, I wasn't sure why it was so important for me to keep this particular copy, but a nagging tug in my gut told me she wouldn't be able to replace it when she tried.

"Okay." She shrugged. "That'll be $37.50."

"For this tiny thing?" I scoffed, ready to pay whatever it took.

"Yes, ma'am. It's our only copy and apparently very valuable." She winked.

"No problem. Here you go." I handed over two twenties. "Keep the change." I laughed. "I've always wanted to say that."

Keelyn snickered and punched a few more keys. "All right, you're all set on computer three."

I looked to the bank of old-school computers lining the far wall. "Actually, can I have number five instead?"

Shaking her head, Keelyn smiled and honored my request. "Of course. Good luck with your research, Milly, and let me know if you need anything else."

I dipped my head. "Thank you. I will."

Tucked into the farthest corner on the first floor, I laid out my notepad, pen, and my personal copy of *The Queen of Nightmares* and poured myself another cup of tea. I needed to stay alert if I was going to get anywhere with this today.

I typed in *Genevieve DuWant* and immediately got a list of all her available books. They ranged from dreamology to psychic powers to *Building a Bridge within Your Mind's Eye*. But Keelyn was right. *The Queen of Nightmares* was the only fiction book she'd ever written, but to me, it contained the most truth of all.

20

CRANING MY NECK, I STRETCHED THE TIGHT muscles, regretting not bringing my pain-relieving cream with me. Three hours and I had no new information on Genevieve DuWant or her kids. A few people had filtered in and out of the library since it opened, but I was still alone enough to cast my spell.

Seven crosses, seven times. Betwixt and between and intertwined. Show me the tree that spawned from thee. Blood to blood, so mote it be.

Ms. DuWant's author bio included her seven children, so I figured this was as good a place as any to start. I'd laid a copy of a US map on the table and sprinkled it with some of the black salt I always kept in my bag. Staring excitedly, I watched the granules move across the parchment, settling in mounds on four different places. That meant three of her children were either no longer with us or resided overseas.

I leaned down to find the one closest to me.

Tapping a finger to the spot, I wrote down the name of the town on my notepad: Augusta, Maine.

I typed the destination into the computer, smiling as I read about the quaint little town. A route came up on the screen, mapping the distance between here and there. It was only three and a half hours away. I still didn't have a name to go on but figured I could use another locater spell once I got there to narrow things down.

Sitting up, I rolled my neck and stretched my back again, my eyes landing on a dark shadow in the corner.

Roarke stepped out from behind the nearest stack, still dressed in all black but in modern clothes and without his cloak.

"Fancy meeting you here." He dropped into the seat beside me, as real as any other person in the library today.

"What are you doing here?" I shifted the map to hide my open book and notepad, swiping the discarded salt onto the floor.

"Yes, well, when my queen doesn't show up in the dreamscape all night, I'm forced to hop over to make sure she's okay." His voice remained light, but I didn't miss the twitch in his jaw or the tension hidden beneath his words.

"I'm sorry. I had some… important things to do. Besides, I didn't realize my presence was required every single night." I shifted in my seat, crossing my arms over my chest.

I didn't want to start a fight, especially with Keelyn's eyes plastered on the two of us from across the room. She dipped her head, raising a brow in appreciation as she eyed Roarke like a hawk.

I smiled and gave her a little shrug, hoping she'd leave us alone.

Turning back to Roarke, I held his gaze, waiting to hear how much trouble I'd caused.

"Hi. I'm Keelyn, head librarian here. And you are?" Keelyn's arm jutted past my shoulder, aiming directly for Roarke.

"Hello. It's nice to meet you." He shook her outstretched hand but didn't offer his name.

Luckily, Keelyn didn't seem to notice. "I haven't seen you here before. Are you a friend of Milly's?"

Roarke looked to me, giving me a chance to spin whatever story I wanted.

"He is. Yes. An old family friend from out of town." I lied.

Keelyn's eyes held mine, her ice-blue stare shooting daggers of doubt straight into my veins.

A beat of silence hung in the air, then... "Well, any friend of Milly's is a friend of mine. Again, it's nice to meet you." Keelyn turned and walked back to her desk without another word. Though, lord knew I'd probably hear about this later.

"So what are these important things you needed to take care of?" Roarke's gaze drifted to the table and the papers in front of me, settling on the computer screen. "What's in Augusta, Maine?"

Panicked, I reeled back through the text I'd read about the town. "Merkaba Sol," I blurted out.

"What?"

"Merkaba Sol. It's a great metaphysical shop Mama used to take me to when I was little. I'm in need of a few important supplies and had to double-check if they had them in stock."

My muscles tightened, the lie causing them to cramp as I internally cringed. I was back to praying the Weaver couldn't read my mind.

Roarke leaned in, whispering in my ear. "You know we could

[157]

just visit in the dreamscape, and I can will you back anything you need."

I thought about his offer, wondering when the last time was that he paid for anything in the real world.

"I'm good. Thanks. I should be there and back by later tonight. So I'll see you then…" I let the words hang in the air, hoping he bought my excuse.

Roarke remained close, tucking a strand of my dark-auburn hair behind my ear. "See you then."

I reached up, feeling something in my hair, and plucked out a miniature rose. I stared at his back as he walked out the front door, knowing he'd disappear as soon as he reached the shadows.

Keelyn was in my face a second later. "Seriously, how could you keep something like this from me? Why did you never mention you had a drop-dead gorgeous friend before?" She plopped down in his vacated chair, waiting for me to explain.

The lie coated my tongue, but the words slid easily enough past my lips. "He's the son of a longtime friend of my mother's and was only in town for a few days. He just stopped by to tell me he was leaving."

Keelyn cocked her head. "How did he know you were here?"

My mouth gaped, the same question ringing in my ears. *How* did *he track me to the library?*

"Milly?" Keelyn's voice roused me again.

"Yeah, I'm not really sure. He probably just remembered the library was the only other place I'd spent time as a kid."

It sounded plausible enough, but I wasn't sure she was buying it.

Finally, she winked. "Well, next time he comes to town, you better invite me to dinner." She stood from the chair, walking away with a skip in her step.

Relieved the interrogations were over, I stared at the tiny flower in my hand, trying to figure out how to get to Augusta and back before nightfall.

The bus would take too long, and I didn't own a car. So…

I stood and gathered my things, signing out of the computer and walking back to the front desk.

"Done already?" Keelyn asked.

I smiled and nodded confidently despite the fact I was trembling inside. "May I ask you a favor?" I tugged the strap of my shoulder bag tighter, needing somewhere to put my hands.

"Sure. How can I help?"

I inhaled sharply, then spewed my request. "I need to borrow your car for the rest of the day."

21

KEELYN'S BRIGHT-BLUE VOLKSWAGEN BUG WAS easy to drive, and I was beyond grateful since this was only my fourth time behind a wheel. Mama tried to teach me a couple of times when I was younger, but after our car was stolen in a neighboring town while we attended the farmers market there, she never replaced it. After that, we only sold our products close to home and never ventured anywhere we couldn't get to by foot or bus. It was then the townsfolk started calling us hermits and other supposedly unflattering names. Personally, at thirteen years old, I thought it was pretty cool I got to stay home helping Mama work in the garden all day. But to the kids in town, it was their first sign that I was a freak. Thankfully, Peter O'Toolle completed my training, teaching me how to drive his father's old truck a few years later—another first we'd shared.

I steered Keelyn's Bug toward the middle of town, parking next to a sprawling green park. The hills rolled out in waves, cutting the landscape into different sections. To the left were picnic tables and barbecue grills, and over the hill to the right were multiple sets of swings and slides. Even though today's temperatures were on the chilly side, laughter filled the air as kids ran and played with their parents seated nearby.

I walked to a vacant table beneath a pavilion and spread out my things: the book, my notes, a map of Augusta I'd bought at the gas station on my way into town, and of course, another vial of black salt.

Running a finger over Genevieve's name, I repeated my spell from before, altering it just a bit.

Seven crosses, seven times. Betwixt and between and intertwined. Show me the one who lives nearby. Blood to blood, let your spirit fly.

Instead of pouring the salt onto the map, I tossed it into the air, waiting for it to drop and settle on a specific spot. Instead, a gust of wind blew through the pavilion, knocking the salt and the rest of my things haphazardly to the ground.

"Shit." I retrieved the items, spreading them flat and trying again.

Seven crosses, seven times. Betwixt and between and intertwined. Show me the one who lives nearby. Blood to blood let your spirit fly.

Another gust and another failure. What in the world was going on?

I gathered my things and rearranged them, needing to try at least one more time to adhere to the rule of three.

With a pinch of salt in my hand, I repeated my spell.

Seven crosses, seven times. Betwixt and between and intertwined. Show me the one who lives nearby. Blood to blood let your spirit fly.

This time, I blew the salt into the air, focusing the magic with the power of my breath.

The tiny black grains whirled before me, spinning themselves into a vortex before dropping into a collected heap atop the map. I bent down, noting the exact location before another gust blew it away.

Identifying the park I was currently in, I traced a finger down streets and around the curved lines that would lead me to the relative of Ms. DuWant. It wasn't far from here, maybe fifteen minutes, so now all I needed to do was figure out what to say.

First, I hoped they would confirm their mother's pseudonym and provide their real last name. Then, I prayed they could identify her source and, if so, be willing to share it with me, a complete stranger.

Shaking my head, I realized how ridiculous this was. Like they would just spill the family secrets. I sat back down on the bench, dropping my head into my hands. Why in the world had I thought this would work?

"Trust your magic, Milly. The goddess will never let you down."

Mama's words floated to my ears, carried this time on a soft wisp of wind.

I lifted my head, looking out to the sky, and saw puffy white clouds meandering across the pristine blue expanse. They filled me with memories of lying in the grass next to my mom. Did I trust my magic at this point? I wasn't entirely sure. But I did trust my mother and all the wisdom she'd imparted to me.

I shoved my things into my bag, carrying them on rushed feet back to Keelyn's car. A quarter mile down the road, then two lefts and a right, and I should arrive at my destination. And Mama was right—I could call on my magic to achieve my goal if necessary.

Veering back into traffic, I felt confident again, bolstered by the memory of my mother's words. As I was growing up, she'd always known exactly what to say to help me through whatever issue I was facing at the time. I suppose that's just what moms do, but somehow her timely musing seemed special. Intuitive even. And that was where the magic came in.

Twelve minutes later, I pulled into the parking lot of the designated spot my spell had indicated and laughed like a fool. Above the door of the square redbrick building hung the sign:

PIKE METAPHYSICAL
- BOOKS, CANDLES, & MORE -

It should have come as no surprise, seeing as Ms. DuWant's literary tendencies had always centered around the occult. But for some reason, I hadn't pictured this.

The indie bookstore was clean and structured with rows of books lining the walls, all labeled accordingly on whitewashed shelves. In the divination section, separate areas had been created for tarot, I Ching, and pendulums, while a nearby shelf held crystal balls and black gazing mirrors in a variety of sizes. Candles were interspersed throughout the store, and the scent of incense hung thickly in the air, giving the shop its overall metaphysical vibe. The building was much smaller than the other I'd read about online, Merkaba Sol, but I tended to prefer this intimate approach, finding it rather charming.

"Hello. Can I help you find something?" A gentle voice sounded from over my shoulder, and I spun around.

A woman perhaps in her midthirties greeted me with a smile. "Welcome to Pike Metaphysical. I'm Isabelle Pike." Bright-green eyes met mine, urging me to speak.

"Hello. Hi," I stammered. "I'm… just passing through and saw your store and thought perhaps you could help me with something."

Isabelle walked closer, her jet-black hair stick straight and hanging slightly below her shoulders. "I'll be happy to try."

I eased the small black book from my bag, my fingers gripping it tightly as I held it up for her to see. "This was written by Genevieve DuWant, and while I'm certain that was a pseudonym, I'm hoping you can help me identify her real name." I knew it was a long shot, but I couldn't waste time beating around the bush.

Isabelle's eyes locked on the book, her brows pinching tight. "Where did you get that?"

"Um… my local library back in Rhode Island. Why?"

"May I?" she asked reverently. She held out her hands, trembling and wanting.

My pulse spiked, hammering in my ears as I offered it to her.

The book's diminutive size barely filled both her palms. Balancing it in one hand, she ran a finger over the title, tracing the author's name in slow, even strokes.

"Can you tell me why it's so special?" I asked.

"Because it's the only copy of the last book my mother ever wrote."

22

OVER THE LAST HOUR, I FOUND OUT Isabelle Pike was Genevieve *Pike's* daughter and the owner of this beautiful bookstore.

"My mother chose to use a pseudonym to keep her author life separate from all us kids. She didn't want anyone targeting us because of what she wrote about."

"I see. But I'm curious as to why there is only one copy of this book. It seems odd that after having so many successful titles published, there wouldn't have been more printed of this one too."

"It was Mother's choice. Her final request actually." Isabelle looked down to the book, which rested safely back in my own hands. "She said that it was special, but none of us ever truly understood why."

My thumb grazed the embossed lettering. *I know why.*

"I'm so glad someone found it, though, and think she would be pleased it was you." Isabelle offered me another cup of tea from the dainty porcelain set she'd brought out earlier from the back of the store.

"Thank you, but I have to be going soon. I do have one more question if that's okay."

"Of course." Isabelle set down the teapot and reclaimed her seat on the couch across from me.

"In the book, your mom refers to using a source. Someone who gave her firsthand information about the subject matter. Do you happen to know who that is… or was?" I amended in case they were no longer alive.

Her eyes caught mine, squinting and contemplative. "I'm sorry, but no. I don't have a clue."

The flames of the nearby candles gutted in an unseen wind. I instinctively drew the book close to my chest and stood to gather my things.

"Well, thank you for your time, Isabelle. It was an absolute pleasure meeting you." I smiled but didn't shake her hand before leaving the store.

She watched me from behind the glass door, giving a little wave as I climbed into Keelyn's car. I wasn't sure why I got nervous all of a sudden, but my witch's instincts told me it was time to go.

Four hours later, I'd returned Keelyn's car and rushed home through the woods, happy to be back on my familiar, foot-worn trail. Today was a victory, even if I didn't get all the answers I wanted. I had left my land, venturing out on my own farther than I ever had before and found myself connecting to a stranger in a pleasant and real way. It was something I'd rarely experienced in my life so far. Perhaps it had to do with where I was and Isabelle's own history with the supernatural, but I didn't feel strange or ostracized while talking about the magical book. My connection with Roarke was spun in the stars, but having someone who understood me and who I could have an honest conversation with here in the real world felt pretty damn good—despite my awkward exit.

My mind relived the moment the entire drive home, searching for the trigger that sent me fleeing the shop. I didn't feel as though Isabelle was keeping anything from me, but again, I couldn't deny the pull in my gut that our conversation had come to a definitive and strange end.

Tomorrow I would start my search anew, looking for anything to do with Genevieve Pike. But tonight, I needed to figure out how I was going to handle Roarke. I wasn't sure if he bought my excuse from earlier today, but I was determined to stand my ground. I might be his chosen queen, but I wasn't at his beck and call. I tucked the small rose into my memory circle, then took my time making dinner and enjoying some cuddle time with Jenks before eventually heading to bed.

Waking to another starlit sky, I spun to get my bearings. Roarke was nowhere in the immediate vicinity as far as I could tell, and based on the strange monolithic mountain standing in the distance, I'd arrived somewhere I'd never been before.

"Roarke?" I called out, receiving no response. I cupped my hands around my mouth and tried again, shouting into the void. "Roarke, are you here?"

A rip opened up in the sky above the towering red mountain. Purple, blue, and magenta stars poured into its center like the entire cosmos was being funneled into its core.

I stood awestruck as a square opening carved itself in the stone, creating a door to another world from which Roarke emerged.

Dressed in his traditional garb, the Weaver stalked toward me, his face hidden beneath the hood of his thick black cloak. Watching him approach gave me butterflies. In this moment, he exuded confidence—his broad shoulders and strong legs carrying him in my direction, the slight swagger in his step, and the dip of his head. He was like a seductive jungle cat closing in on its prey, and suddenly I wondered if that prey was me. Was he honestly angry that I hadn't shown up for an entire night? At this point, I couldn't tell.

Shifting on my feet, I called out to him, trying to get a feel for where his emotions lay. "Hi." I waved. "Where are we? This place is absolutely amazing."

He remained silent, continuing forward and closing the distance between us.

I knew he wouldn't hurt me, but instinctively, my magic rose to the surface, reacting to my fear. Not that I had a clue if I could defend myself against a Weaver if I had to. *Dammit.* There was still so much I didn't know.

I lowered my hand and stood still, waiting for him to get closer.

[169]

The features of his face finally came into view, and I exhaled a sigh of relief. Silver light shimmered brightly from beneath his hood due to a wide smile that reached his eyes.

"I'm so glad you're here!" He swept me up into a crushing hug, spinning us around.

A laugh bubbled out of me as he set me back on my feet. "Where exactly is here? What is this place?" I pointed to the lone mountain standing in the distance, its top still being flooded with cosmic light.

"This is the Weaver's Gate. It's the source of all of our magic."

Stunned silent, I marveled at the open landscape in front of me, allowing the beauty and grandeur to fully penetrate my being. The power I felt coming from the mountain was beyond words. Intense and almost divine.

Roarke confirmed my suspicions as he explained further. "Mamu is the female goddess of dreams, and Zaqu is her male counterpart who ruled the entire realm. They are the children of the Mesopotamian god Utu and were worshiped all throughout Babylon and Sumer as well. After they ascended, this is where the first Weaver was created."

I stared into the opening of the mountain, imagining Roarke's distant relative being chosen by the gods and forged within.

"This is where your family line originates from?"

Roarke laughed. "We weren't born of the gods, if that's what you're asking. My ancestor was human before he was selected and blessed with Zaqu's power. With the god of dreams no longer present in the realm, he needed a sentinel, or a chosen proxy, to bestow his magic upon." He turned back to the star-filled mountain. "And this is where that transfer began. Every Weaver since then has accepted their magic here, blessed by the gods of old."

I couldn't believe I was standing in the presence of a god-made portal. The sparkling galaxy brightened in the sky as if reacting to my reverence.

"Can we go inside?" The question tumbled from my lips before I could stop it, and the look on Roarke's face had me bracing for some sort of cosmic retribution.

"No, Milly. Only Weavers are allowed inside. And it's important you understand that. Anyone not chosen who enters the gate would be destroyed instantly. Even with our cloaks in place for protection, the energy is beyond anything in this world."

I tilted my head. "Then why did you bring me here?"

I wondered again if this was some sort of punishment for not showing up in the dreamscape last night. Was I divinely required to do so after accepting my role as the Weaver's queen? I wiped my hands down the front of my dress, noticing its unassuming nature for the first time since waking here. Perhaps I was brought here to pay penance. Whether by Roarke or through my own guilt, I wasn't sure.

"I brought you here to answer your questions more fully, Milly. You seem to still be wavering on whether you can trust me or not, and I wanted to prove to you that you can. I don't want to hide anything from you. And sharing the Weaver's origin story and the source of my magic is as vulnerable as it gets."

Again, I sighed in relief, happy with Roarke's confession.

Taking his hand, I took a step forward, bringing us toe to toe. "It's not that I don't trust you, Roarke. It's just that I don't fully understand my role as your queen." He moved to step back, but I stood firm, holding him close. "I know you've explained that there's nothing I need to physically do, but with the random occurrences happening in and out of the dreamscape, I feel like the bad things going on are somehow connected to me." I shared my own confession, then took a step back.

Roarke's eyes grew dark, shifting from silver to a deep cobalt blue, and I immediately regretted revealing my fears.

23

"ROARKE, WHAT'S WRONG? WHAT DID I SAY?" Panic gripped my chest as he grabbed my hand and raced us toward the gate.

Sparks flared high above the mountain's opening, sputtering and spinning cosmic debris back into the sky.

"Come on! Someone is trying to access the gate, and I need to close it now!"

Oh, thank God. This had nothing to do with me. All my assumptions about tonight had been wrong, and I couldn't be more grateful.

Running beside Roarke as fast as I could, we neared the opening in the side of the mountain. A pedestal of some sort sat inside the vast cavern, but that was all I could see through the blinding light radiating from within.

He released my hand and ran inside, leaving me to wait at the mountain's base.

Excruciating moments of not knowing what was going on pulled me closer to the opening until Roarke reappeared and the door to the gods' portal slammed shut, sealing the gate completely. I looked up, relieved when the sky began to clear.

"Is everything okay? Did you close it in time?"

Roarke took my hand and waved his other in the air, transporting us to a new location. The familiar scent of roses and peonies bombarded my senses as he collapsed onto the nearest white metal bench inside the English greenhouse, pulling me down with him.

"Roarke, are you all right?" I scooted closer.

Slumped against the bench, he gasped for air, breathing heavily. I'd never seen him this stressed or exhausted.

"I'm fine. I just need to catch my breath."

I slipped my hand from his and eased off the bench, moving to stand behind a nearby lilac bush, giving him the space I thought he needed.

"Milly, wait. Don't go."

I returned, standing slightly in front of him.

"What happened earlier wasn't your fault."

"I don't think that," I replied, not sure what he meant.

"Well, you said you thought the bad things going on might be connected to you, and I want to make sure you know that wasn't the case. Someone else is trying to access the Weaver magic."

I gasped. "What? How is that even possible?"

He dropped his head into his hands. "I don't know. Nothing like this has ever happened before. But I've been fighting off an outside threat for the past week."

I knelt in front of him, placing my hands on his legs. "I'm sorry. I had no idea. You should have told me, and I could have tried to help."

"It's okay, and I'm not sure there's anything you can do. No one else can enter the gate but me. But I've been having to check on it more and more and wanted to show you so you understood."

I took his hands in mine, pulling us both to our feet. "I do understand. And I'm sorry I wasn't here the other night. It won't happen again."

Pulling from my grasp, he cupped both of my cheeks. "Thank you, Milly. We are definitely stronger together."

His words struck like an arrow, sharp and penetrating and filling me with more guilt. All I'd done since becoming his queen was teeter back and forth, questioning everything, and in the process, weakening our link. A sound escaped my lips, a hollow, regretful cry from the deepest part of my soul.

I froze, listening as it started to rain. Light drops tinkled gently on the glass at first, transforming into an increased pounding like fate hammering its way inside. The sky turned dark, and my fears rolled back into place. Why was this happening again? Every time I entered the dreamscape, something always seemed to go wrong.

Ominous clouds continued to build, turning the usually vibrant greenhouse into a stark, eerie, vine-filled place.

"I think we should go," I confessed, nervous that a literal dark cloud was somehow following me.

Roarke waved his hand, and we stepped out into his forest once more. Frigid air nipped at my hands and face, but it was a natural temperature for the location, nothing strange or out of place. We hurried down the path to his cabin, and once inside, I made him some tea.

"Are you feeling any better?" I asked.

Roarke sipped the healing blend, nodding slowly. "Yes. Thank you so much. Closing the gate in such a rapid way takes more energy than I'm used to expending, but I'll be fine."

I wrapped my arms around my middle. It was the first time I'd ever seen Roarke affected by anything, and it scared me. "Do you know who is trying to access your magic?"

He shook his head, taking another swig of tea. "I have no idea."

I paced the kitchen, not sure what to do with myself. "Besides monitoring the gate, is there anything else we can do?"

Roarke's smile warmed. "Not that I know of. *We* just need to remain vigilant."

I realized he was smiling because I included myself in the offer to help. And I wanted to. But as usual, I had no idea what to do. "What do you mean remain vigilant?"

"Just that we need to check on the gate daily and that our united presence will be needed in the dreamscape every night."

My gaze dropped to the floor. He didn't say he was upset by my absence the other night, but clearly it was an issue. "I already told you it won't happen again."

Roarke set down his cup and joined me in the kitchen, taking my hands in his. "Milly, as we talked about before, our combined magic will work in the dreamscape with or without you here. But I won't lie. We are stronger together. So until I figure out what's going on, it's simply the safest bet."

"Like... I need to stay here? Twenty-four hours a day? Won't that cause a problem with my body in the real world?" I thought back to Jenks's angry yowls after I'd slept for so long and wondered if his fear was for himself or for me.

"Normally, yes, a human body would atrophy and starve if not taken care of for long periods of time, but since you are my chosen queen, being here affects you differently. So you don't have to worry. Nothing can harm your body in the real world as long as you're with me."

I knew his words were meant to comfort, but instead, a raging panic seeped deep into my bones. "Roarke, I can't stay here all the time. I have a life to maintain in the real world too." I pulled my hands from his, walking to stare out over the lake through the floor-to-ceiling windows at the back of the house.

The water calmed me but only slightly. Tonight its dark water churned with waves. Just like me. "I'll be here every night, I swear. It's the best I can offer, and I hope you understand."

Roarke's presence hovered directly behind me, his energy pressing against mine even though he didn't reach out. "I understand. I'll see you tomorrow night."

I turned around, ready to explain that I didn't need to leave right now, but all I saw was Roarke's back retreating out the front door.

I ran after him, my feet pounding against the cold, hard dirt, but I couldn't catch up. By the time I reached the clearing, he was gone.

I spun around, not sure what to do. He could have gone *literally* anywhere, and I had no idea how to find him. Or how to make amends. It seemed all I'd done since becoming his queen was upset the balance in some way—the complete opposite of what I was supposed to do.

Closing my eyes, I let my head fall back and listened to the wind. Blowing through the evergreens, its gentle whistle was like a siren's song, pulling me back to my hereditary magic within.

A flare of power sparked in my gut, moving upward and into my chest. Energy flowed through my veins, pooling and throbbing all the way to my hands.

I opened my eyes and found the shadows and stars of my Weaver magic sparking to life between my fingers. And with a twitch of recognition, I knew exactly where Roarke had gone.

24

PEERING OUT INTO THE DARK, I SPOTTED Roarke's silhouette at the top of the mountain. This wasn't the Weaver's Gate but instead a wintery wonderland cresting high in the clouds.

"May I join you?" I asked tentatively, not wanting to overstep.

Roarke patted the seat beside him where he sat on a bench near the mountain's edge.

Bundled in winter gear, I shuffled through the snow. I sat down, remaining silent as I took in the mesmerizing view. Stars shined brightly, hanging high in the night sky, while far below glowed the lights of a glittering town. "Where are we?"

"The top of Pike's Peak," Roarke replied without diverting his eyes. "Did you know this is where Katharine Bates wrote 'America the Beautiful'?"

"No, I didn't."

"It's said she stood here for only thirty minutes in the summer of 1893, and it was all the inspiration she needed to write the patriotic poem." Roarke turned to look at me, his face highlighted in the moonlight. "She wrote it as a kind of prayer for a country that had lost its way."

I recalled the lyrics and fought the rising lump in my throat. "That's beautiful."

"I was here, you know? In 1893."

I recalled Roarke's timeline, remembering he'd accepted his role a hundred and seventy-five years ago. "Do you mean to say you had a hand in her inspiration?"

My smile faded when he turned away, his eyes breaking from mine. "No. In reality, she seemed really sad."

"Is that why you return here when you're sad?" I guessed.

He nodded slowly, leaning down to pick a flower beside his boot. "I figure if something so beautiful could come out of someone's sadness here, it's the perfect place to ease my heart as well."

He handed me the tiny arctic yellow violet, and I gazed out from the peak, losing myself in the night sky as I imagined the stars as the hopes and dreams of all the residents below.

Pike's Peak marked the western edge of Colorado Springs, and my mind caught on the name. It was the same as Genevieve's true surname, though I doubted there was any relation. Still, I couldn't lose sight of what I had planned. I needed to locate her source if I had any chance of breaking Roarke's curse.

My mouth opened, ready to confess what I knew, but the words died on my tongue when Roarke leaned over and laid his head in my lap.

I think I'd loved Roarke since the first time I saw him in my dreams. I didn't know how it happened—destiny, loneliness, or a combination of the two—but since then, my days had been colored with the hope of it, lighting a path leading forever back to him.

I couldn't tell him he was cursed when he was already so upset. And now, even more so, I planned to take care of it myself.

We sat beneath the stars for hours, protected from the elements by our Weaver magic. Roarke eventually stood, pulling me up for a kiss, then transported us back to his home. The cabin was toasty. Warmed by the fire to the perfect degree. He released my hand, walking straight to the bedroom. A moment later, the fall of water hit the slate tiles of his shower floor.

I turned to go, feeling as though he might need time alone, when suddenly warm water sprayed my back.

Roarke's hands settled on my bare shoulders, his husky voice whispering in my ear. "I need you, Milly. Will you stay?"

I stood frozen. Momentarily mortified as years of shyness held me in place. Roarke's hands didn't move. He waited patiently for the answer that would shape our night.

I gathered my courage and spun to face him, baring myself, soul and all. "Of course I'll stay."

Our lips crashed together. Roarke's mouth seared mine beneath the hot water as his hands started to roam. Slipping across my skin, he followed the curves from my shoulders to my hips, reaching around to cup my backside in both hands.

"Have I told you how gorgeous you are?" he whispered, his tongue licking the side of my neck.

I tilted my head, giving him full access. "No, but... thank you. I—" A moan escaped me, cutting off my words. Roarke's fingers found their way between my legs, and I lost all sense of thoughts or speech.

Lost in each other, I let myself drift beneath the water and into his strong arms.

The energy between us was undeniable. And Roarke was right. The magic we created had the power to change the world—starting with my own.

Never before had I felt so wanted. So sexy or loved. The emotions of our connection threatened to overwhelm me until Roarke cupped the back of my head, placing his forehead against mine.

"Milly, I love you so much."

I took a deep breath, my heart racing and wild. "I love you too, Roarke."

With our shared words, the night came undone.

I woke the next morning still wrapped in Roarke's arms but was anxious to get home. I had a gut feeling I needed to follow, and if I was right, it couldn't wait.

Leaning in, I placed a kiss on his cheek. "I have to go."

He didn't wake and barely moved when I eased out of bed, still exhausted from what happened at the gate.

Dressed, I headed outside and back down the path to the clearing. Waving my hand like I'd seen Roarke do so many times, I created a rip in space and stepped through. Once off his hidden island and back in the dreamscape, I'd wake up in the real world, and then it was time to get to work.

I wasn't sure if Isabelle Pike had anything to do with the attack at the gate, but I couldn't shake the odd feeling I got during our initial conversation. And since she was the only lead I had concerning the curse, I figured it was the best place to start.

Jenks nuzzled my nose as I woke up back in my cottage, happy to see me and ready for his food.

"Good morning, sweet boy. I'm happy to see you too."

Smiling, I jumped up and added the yellow violet to my memory circle, then started the process of feeding us both.

Now showered and dressed for the day, I packed a bag and bid Jenks goodbye with a scratch behind his ears. Racing down the path to the library, I hoped Keelyn would let me borrow her car again.

"Hey there! You're certainly up early. All bright-eyed and bushy-tailed." Keelyn laughed at her own joke as she pushed the cart of recently returned books into the stacks.

"Good morning. Yes, I actually came by early to see if I could borrow your car again. I need to head back to Maine to do some more research." The urgency I was feeling pushed me to get straight to the point.

"Does this have anything to do with the book I found for you?"

I cocked my head. Keelyn hardly ever asked me questions about my books.

"Yes. Why?"

"No reason. I just thought it was odd that after you bought the only copy we had, I was unable to order another. In fact"—she stopped and turned to face me—"I found out there were only two copies printed in the entire world, and I'm thinking I should have charged you more." Her wide smile indicated she was teasing, but her words froze me in place.

Isabelle told me there was only one copy printed, which meant... she lied.

"Wow! Really? That is strange. Well, if you'd like me to pay a little more, just let me know."

"No, no. I'm only teasing. And to answer your question... yes, you can borrow my car." She dug into the pocket of her pinstriped skirt and handed me the keys. "Happy hunting."

"Thanks!"

That was exactly what I was going to do.

25

FOUR HOURS LATER, I WAS PARKED OUTSIDE Isabelle's shop. I didn't think she would answer any more of my direct questions, which left me with just one alternative—magic.

I'd need to cast a spell that would allow me to see the truth behind her words, and I only hoped she couldn't counteract me. If she was using her mother's book as a guide to connect to the Weaver's magic, that meant she must be a practicing witch as well.

I pulled out a sachet containing the herbs I'd used in my original truth spell against Roarke and poured them into the steaming cup of green tea I stopped for along the way.

Reveal the truth. Allow me to see. Magic being hidden from me. Open my heart and my mind's eye. Show me the truth of Pike's fine lie.

The goddess's energy filled the car, setting my blood alight. Hopefully, with a few well-placed questions, my suspicions would be put to rest. Clutching my bag to my side, I entered the shop, more nervous than I'd ever been.

"Milly! You're back. It's nice to see you again so soon." Isabelle emerged from the back room with a large stack of books about to topple from her arms.

I rushed forward. "Here, let me help you." Taking the top few, I placed them on the nearby table and stood back.

"Thank you so much. I thought I had them right up until the end." Isabelle laughed, gesturing for me to take a seat on the couch. "What brings you back to my neck of the woods?"

I opened my mouth, but nothing came out. I had no idea how to ask these questions without offending her or showing my hand. "Uh… I just wondered… umm…" I stammered.

"What is it, Milly? You can ask me anything."

Wringing my hands in my lap, I finally blurted out, "I was just wondering if you were a witch."

Isabelle's eyes narrowed. Then the store filled with her boisterous laugh. "That's why you were nervous? To ask me if I was a witch?" She flung her arms out wide. "You've read my mother's books, and just look around… Of course I am."

It was so strange to hear such an open confession, seeing as Mama had always taught me to keep my gifts a secret.

"Bide the Wiccan Laws we must. In perfect love and perfect trust. Soft of eye and light of touch. Speak little and listen much."

Mama often repeated those lines of the Wiccan Rede to me as a child. Along with the ideals of the witch's pyramid: To know. To dare. To will. And to keep silent.

"These are the traits witches have lived by for centuries, and we will not dishonor them in this home. Our magic is a gift from the goddess, Milly. And for that blessing, we keep it ours alone."

"I've just never met a witch who was so open about her gifts," I admitted.

"Yes, well, when your craft is part of your livelihood, it's hard to keep it a secret."

"I suppose you're right." I smiled, my spell not picking up any twists to her words.

"Do you practice?" she asked in return.

"Um… I only tend my gardens," I replied, practically freezing up again.

"Herbal magic is nothing to shake your head at. Again, I'm glad you found me and are a fan of my mother's work. I know she would have appreciated meeting you."

"Were you involved with any of your mother's research?" I pressed on, hoping the flow of our conversation seemed natural to her.

Isabelle paused, then answered, "No. Like I said before, she chose to keep her work separate from us kids." Her lips closed into a hard line, and my spell formed a tight knot within my chest.

She was lying, and I knew it had to do with my little black book.

"I can understand that. I did have another question about the book I showed you before. You said it was the only copy, but I couldn't find the publisher or printer's information inside and wondered if you might be able to share that with me."

It was a risk to discuss the book directly, but I saw no other way to veer my questions toward the Weaver or her knowledge of him.

Isabelle's back straightened, and my insides turned to mush. I'd never been in a confrontation with another witch before, and I had no idea who would come out on top. I hoped my own magic would be strong enough, but if I had to, I knew I could pull on the Weaver's magic as well.

"I'm sorry. I don't actually know. I was so little back then, being the youngest of all my siblings."

No tightness formed in my gut, meaning she was telling the truth.

"But you're sure there was only one copy produced?"

She squinted again. "I'm sure."

"*Ugh*," I moaned, grabbing my stomach, the force of her lie bending me in half.

"Are you all right?"

I nodded and spun an excuse. "I'm fine but probably should have passed on that breakfast burrito from the gas station this morning."

She knew there was another copy, and I had no doubt she was using it to try to gain access to Roarke's magic.

Recovering, I sat up. "Well, thank you for answering my questions. I suppose I should let you get back to work now."

"Stay," she snapped, then smoothed her tone. "I just have to shelve these books and refill some of the crystal bins, but then we could grab an early lunch if you'd like."

I had no desire to stick around but thought perhaps if I spent a little more time with her, she might open up… or slip up, revealing something I could use. "Great. That sounds fun. Would you like some help shelving the books?"

"No. I've got it. You just relax or have a look around. Actually, I just got in a new shipment of dried flowers and herbs. I'd love for you to take a look at them and give me your opinion."

"Um… sure." I wasn't sure how my opinion would matter, but this gave me another idea of how I could sell my wares back home.

We didn't have a metaphysical store in West Greenwich, but I knew of one a couple towns away that might be willing to work out a deal.

Isabelle guided me to her stockroom, pointing to the crates of packaged herbs in the corner. "Let me know what you think of the quality." With a wink, she left me alone in the room.

Boxes holding books, candles, oils, and herbs were stacked neatly in sections, all ready to be moved out front and put on sale. I couldn't help but think of my small storeroom back home with cabinets full of my handmade creams, herbal blends, and teas. I didn't see anything like that here and wondered if I should offer them to Isabelle. If she agreed to consign some of my things, it would be an easy way for me to keep an eye on her without arousing any further suspicion… *hopefully*.

I opened one of the herb packets and inspected the dried seed pods inside. The quality was okay, if a little stagnant, but I wasn't about to offer such a big-yield item and be forced to grow and harvest just to fulfill her stock.

I walked back into the front room, sharing my thoughts. "Your herb packets look good, but I was wondering—"

I froze, staring at Isabelle's eyes as they glowed a sickly yellow-green. Her black hair was blowing wildly in the air as if an unseen tornado had formed inside the shop. However, the most disturbing thing about the scene was her insidious smile as she waved my little black book held tightly in her hand.

"Isabelle, what are you doing?" I shouted.

"It should have been me." Her voice was raw and strained, screaming above the magical wind tearing through her store.

Shelves were upended, spilling their contents onto the floor. Books flew across the room like in a real-life horror film, and the closer I got, the more I could feel the tainted magic she was using to pierce the dreamscape's veil.

"Stop. You have no idea what you're doing." I threw out my hand, knocking her off balance with a powerful blast of my own. My hereditary magic flowed through me, giving me the strength and wisdom in this time of need. The energy surged, culminating in a shock wave that shook the walls and brought Isabelle to her knees.

"You don't deserve it…" Isabelle stammered, weeping from the floor.

"What are you talking about?"

She looked up at me, her eyes still glowing that putrid yellow-green. "I should be his Queen of Nightmares! Not you."

26

SHOCKED BY HER ADMISSION, I FLUNG MY arms wide, then squeezed my hands back together to bind her in place. "What do you mean it should be you? Explain. Now!"

"My mother knew all about his world... the *Weaver* and his partner. I've studied her writings for years, all so I could find him within my dreams and become his Queen of Nightmares. But then he found you," she spat. "I knew the moment he'd chosen someone else. I could feel it ripple through the night, smashing all my hopes and dreams." She dropped her head. "I could tell it was you the moment you stepped into my store. But you don't deserve the title. From what you've shared, you're too much of a goody-two-shoes to accept that your part of the magic is what brings people's nightmares to life." She lifted her head, her yellow-green eyes flaring again. "Don't tell me you didn't notice the bad things happening in the dreamscape after you accepted your role. You can't possibly be that naive."

I gasped, my hold on her waning. She'd hit the core of my deepest, darkest fear. I had read what the book said about the Queen of Nightmares but refused to believe it was coming from me. Roarke wouldn't have purposely turned my magic dark to balance out his own. It simply couldn't be true.

"You're lying." I tightened my grip on her again, holding her in place.

"I'm not, and I think deep down you know it. You're not cut out to be his queen."

"What, and you are?" I snapped back.

"Yes! My mother might not have been a Weaver or his queen, but she knew all about him, and that makes me far more prepared than you." She cocked her head. "So why don't you crawl back home to your hidey-hole in Rhode Island and relinquish your title and Weaver magic to me?"

Relinquish my Weaver magic? I'd cringed at the thought before, but it was still my choice—to remain Roarke's Queen of Nightmares or to simply walk away. He'd always told me it was up to me. My decision as to whether I wanted this life or not. And so far, I had. I'd chosen yes to all he offered. But now, with Isabelle confirming my fears, I wasn't so sure. Could I really enter the dreamscape every night, knowing I was truly the cause of everything bad that happened there?

My chest heaved, my breathing turning rapid and shallow. I wasn't sure I could do this anymore. Honestly, I knew I couldn't. I simply wasn't strong enough to deal with the guilt.

"Fine. But even if I walk away, it doesn't mean you will automatically become his queen. There are plenty of other witches out there that are stronger and more deserving than you."

Isabelle watched me through her power-fueled eyes, her head tilting from side to side. "Why do you think I've been testing the gate? Once my energy has been recognized there, it will only take you stepping down for me to become his new queen."

I suspected she had been the one trying to access the Weaver's magic, but my thoughts on why had been completely wrong. I thought she simply wanted the power for herself, but in reality, she wanted the gods to recognize her as his rightful queen.

I thought about Roarke and how he was going to process all this, and a tear rolled down my cheek.

"Aww, don't cry. It won't hurt a bit. All you have to do is tell your Weaver that you've chosen to walk away, and just like that, you'll be stripped of your connection and can go back to living your normal, fairy-tale life."

I peered into Isabelle's sick eyes, oddly crushed that she turned out to be such a vicious, mean-hearted person. "Your mother would be ashamed of you."

I fell forward, a hard yank tugging at my control.

Isabelle stood, fighting with all she had against my magic. "How dare you speak of her? Just because you read a few books she wrote doesn't mean you knew her at all. She was always so protective of her information and her sources. None of us kids were ever interesting enough to occupy her time. But as I grew older, I read her books and studied all the things she had offered to the public but not me. And I grew strong. I honed my own brand of magic and carved out a spot in her world just for me. And even then... she couldn't even say she was proud of me before she died. Just that she loved us all and to stay protected and safe in this crazy, unpredictable world."

She took a step forward, fighting through my spell. "That was it! Just love you… Stay safe. Not here are the tools you need to change the world. Or, Isabelle, you can be so much more…" She trailed off, looking around her shop, lost in the despair of her mother's contempt.

But I didn't think that was what it was.

"Isabelle, you may think she didn't care, but the fact that she protected you from this world proves that she did. Magic comes with a price, and maybe she just couldn't stand the thought of any of you having to pay that."

She scoffed. "That's easy for you to say. You're a hereditary witch. Blessed by your ancestors and bound to carry on their magic with no price at all."

"I lost my mother too!" I screamed. "That's price enough!"

Isabelle fought against my magic, step after step, until she was halfway across the floor. With one final push, I bound her again, dropping her back to her knees. Grabbing my bag and book, I raced out of the shop, her cries echoing behind me.

"Walk away, Milly. I'll be waiting to take your place."

I burst into the library three and a half hours later, dropping to the floor and tossing Keelyn's keys away.

"Milly, honey, my god! What's wrong? Are you okay?" Keelyn rushed to my side, picking me up and shuffling us into a nearby room.

The long, wood meeting table was shiny and polished, gleaming and welcoming, which made me cry even harder.

"Honey, please calm down. Have a seat." Keelyn eased me into the nearest chair, kneeling to wipe the tears from my cheeks. "Okay. Now take a deep breath and tell me what's happened."

I looked up into her ice-blue eyes, and my heart broke a little more. "I can't. You wouldn't understand."

She picked up my hand, giving it a squeeze. "Is this about that friend that came to visit?" She guessed.

I nodded my head, not wanting to face the truth.

"Oh, sweetie. Did you guys break up?"

"I'm not sure if we were ever truly together," I blurted out.

Keelyn stiffened. "Did he hurt you? Take advantage of you?"

Gasping past my sobs, I answered brokenly, "No... Nothing... like that. I... wanted him. But... I can't—" I couldn't push out the rest of the words, dropping my head into my hands.

"Oh, Milly." She rubbed a motherly hand down my back. "We've all been there—wanting someone we can't have. You'll be okay, honey. You'll find someone else the minute you're not looking.

At the grocery store or one of your farmers markets. Heck… you could even meet someone right here."

I lifted my head and wiped my eyes. She had no idea, but Keelyn just set me on my new life's purpose.

I would break this damn curse. Then Roarke and I could be together in the real world, despite his new *queen*.

27

THE ONE THING ISABELLE CONFIRMED IN ALL her rantings was that her family was not related to Agitha, the witch who cast the original curse. Whether I believed her or not, it unfortunately put me back at square one.

I needed to talk to Roarke about all this, but I wasn't ready. There was so much to consider and process. Staying awake and studying through the night would have been my choice, but I couldn't let him down again. I swore I'd return every night to help him protect the gate, but now… knowing where the threat was coming from, perhaps I could do more from out here.

If I cast a binding spell on Isabelle in the real world, maybe she wouldn't continue to attack the gate in the dreamscape, offering Roarke a break. And maybe I could buy myself some more time before I had to see him again.

I went to the kitchen to make more tea, but this tea wasn't for a spell. It was the kind of tea you barely sipped at until it went cold while you cried your eyes out. I hadn't made many pots like it in the past but had a feeling with everything going on, it wouldn't be my last.

I was heartbroken by all I'd learned and what I might be forced to do. Because Isabelle was right. I wasn't built to bring harm to anyone, and if being the Weaver's Queen of Nightmares truly was how my magic was being used, I simply didn't have a choice. I *would* have to walk away.

Another sob forced its way up, catching in my throat. I looked to the fire, allowing myself this release. But once my tears were shed, it was time to go to work.

Bind her magic, tied to thee. Keep her on this plane, so mote it be.

The spell I cast on Isabelle was simple, but I knew it would work. The locking energy I'd used on her at her shop snapped back into place, and it was as if I could hear her screaming from afar. It wasn't a permanent solution and wouldn't last long, but it gave me the time I needed to dig into the book and Agitha's history once more.

I remixed my "stay awake" herbs, then added them to my last few cups of tea, double-checking the protections around my home. Roarke would be upset I ditched him again, but it was for his own good. Hopefully, he'd understand.

Flipping to the middle of the book, I reread the passages that discussed Agitha and her original curse. There wasn't much information to go on besides her first name and that she was disgruntled because the Weaver of the time hadn't selected her to be his queen. I thought of Isabelle and how upset she was due to the exact same thing and kept circling back to that connection.

"Dammit," I cursed out loud.

The library was closed for the night, but when I could use the computer again, I'd trace the Pike family tree to set my mind at ease, confirming if Isabelle was lying or not. And if she was, she was more important to me than she knew. I would use her bloodline to break the curse. Then it wouldn't matter what happened in the dreamscape because Roarke and I would be together for real.

I no longer doubted that was what I wanted, but now I'd have to fight to get it. And I would fight tooth and nail to make this right for us both. Weaver magic was beyond powerful, and I couldn't deny I was thrilled to have it as part of me. But in reality, it wasn't the magic that pulled at my soul. It was him.

I knew when I walked away that it would feel like a betrayal to him. But I hoped once I explained the curse and what I was trying to do, he would give me the time needed without his feelings toward me changing or fading altogether.

It was a risk I'd have to take.

I had no idea how long we'd be apart or where my research would lead me, but if I had to, I would spend the rest of my life looking for a way to break the curse. But first I needed to utilize my own magic to bring me back to my center. Mama's energy still flowed throughout the house, and whenever I felt off balance, all I had to do was connect with my hereditary magic to feel whole once again.

Stoking the fire, I poured another cup of my "stay awake" tea and settled on the floor. Cross-legged, I stared into the flames, imagining my mom and what she might have to say.

A warmth that went beyond the flames enveloped me, comforting me like one of her hugs.

"Mama, I need your help. For the first time in my life, I've fallen in love. But the relationship is not without hurdles. It will force me out into the world alone, farther than I've ever been before. And to be honest, I think that's what scares me the most." A lump formed in my throat. "I wish you were here."

I spent the rest of the night communing with Mama's memory before the flames, settling on my plans by the time the sun rose in the sky.

Keelyn's bright smile was a welcome sight when I stepped inside the library minutes after it opened.

"Good morning, Milly. Back so soon? I've been so worried about you. Are you sure you're okay?" She stepped out from behind the desk.

I held up my hands. "Yes, and don't worry, I don't need to borrow your car again today," I joked awkwardly, trying to make light of her concern.

She huffed and shook her head. "Don't fret a bit. I didn't mind at all."

"Well, thank you. I truly do appreciate it."

"What brings you in, then?"

"Just some genealogy research I want to do."

Keelyn stiffened. "Genealogy?"

"Yes. I recently met someone and told her I'd help look into her ancestry." I lied again.

Suddenly, it felt invasive and wrong to look into someone's family history without their knowledge. But I didn't have a choice. I had to find out if Isabelle was lying about her heritage and whether she was the key to breaking this curse or not.

"Well, good luck. I set you up on computer five again. Holler if you need anything." Keelyn lowered her voice to a conspiratorial whisper. "Not really, but you know what I mean."

I giggled and walked to the bank of computers, once again taking my preferred seat. With a few strokes of the keys, I typed in Genevieve Pike's name and started to read. A slew of random articles popped up, which I quickly weeded through. Then I focused my search on the New England territories since that was where Isabelle had settled, and based on the way she talked about growing up in the area, it was worth a shot. Twenty minutes later, and after expanding my search to include Pike Metaphysical, I found an obituary mentioning Genevieve and all seven of her children. They had, in fact, originated from Maine, with all but Genevieve and Isabelle moving away after their father died eleven years ago.

Once I had the father's name, I was able to trace back with a little more ease, finally landing on a genealogy page that confirmed

Isabelle's words. The Pikes weren't related to Agitha as far as I could tell, and that put a quick end to my research today.

Returning home, I stomped into the house, startling Jenks with the smack of the door. "Sorry, baby. I'm just so… frustrated." I flopped down onto the couch, my thermos of tea almost empty.

With my familiar curled up in my lap, I let my mind wander. I didn't know what to do, but if I was being honest with myself, I wasn't ready to face Roarke just yet, and I wasn't sure I ever would be. Whether it was his true intention to turn me and my magic dark, I still wasn't sure. But if I fell asleep now, I'd have to tell him about the curse, Isabelle, and that I was choosing to walk away. My chest heaved, exhaustion settling deep in my bones. Obviously, I couldn't stay awake forever, but perhaps if I cast my spell again to walk in the dreamscape alone, I could rest while avoiding that confrontation a little while longer.

Retrieving the smudge stick and the chunk of blue lace agate from my altar, I recreated my spell, focusing on a new destination.

Goddess of night, hear my plea. Shroud me from the one who sees. Let me walk within my dreams, shielded and alone. So mote it be.

I woke to a strange silence, but as a familiar warmth settled around me, I knew my spell had worked. With the Weaver's magic, I was still powerful here, and when I opened my eyes and found myself lying in my own garden with Mama by my side, I knew this was exactly where I needed to be.

28

THE DREAM WAS A SIMPLE CREATION OF my heart and soul, but I didn't care. Lying on a bed of freshly cut grass, I reached out and took my mother's hand.

"The sky is particularly fluffy today. We should be able to spot some great images."

Tears rolled down my cheeks as the nearness of her voice was more than a memory here. I turned my head, peering into her kind green eyes. "I'd be happy to spend all day cloud painting with you."

That's what we used to call it: cloud painting. After a long day's work in the garden, we'd lie in the grass and paint the sky with images we saw in the clouds. There were times I thought it was silly. But I'd give anything to be that little girl again, living a simple life with her mom by her side.

A sweet smile pulled at her lips, and I had to turn away. I could spend forever with her here, and that was a dangerous thing to consider. With the power of the Weaver coursing through my veins, I could return here as often as I wanted, and the idea of walking away suddenly seemed like a mistake.

We spent hours painting the sky, calling out the shapes as they floated in and out of view.

"There! See the panda?" Mom pointed to a particularly poofy cloud.

"I see it!" I laughed, fighting back more tears. "Mama, can I ask you something?"

"Of course, sweet girl. What is it?"

I took a deep breath. "I've met someone, and I love him. But being with him will change me—"

"Stop right there," Mama interrupted, rolling to face me. "Change is inevitable. But the question is: Are you happy with who you are now, or would you be a better version of yourself if you allowed it to occur?"

"I'm not sure. And there's no way to tell. It has to do with our magic and my role as his chosen mate."

"Mate?" She sat up, shaking her head. "A soul bond is a powerful thing. But you need to think about what's right for you, Milly. At your core. Then consider how you would feel about yourself and who you would become if you stayed the course with him." She reached for my hand. "I would tell you to follow your heart, but it can be such a fickle thing. In this case, I think you need to listen to what's in your head and use your goddess-given magic to search within your soul. Only then will the answer be revealed."

It was as if my dreamscape knew what I had to do and was forcing the words through Mama's mouth. I had already searched my soul and knew I couldn't be the one to inflict nightmares upon the world. It simply wasn't who I was or who I wanted to be.

The scene around us flickered, and I knew it was time to go. "Thank you, Mama. I love you so much. This has been the best day I've had in a really long time."

"Oh, sweet girl, I'm always around. Just look to the sky and find me in the clouds."

I closed my eyes as she placed a kiss on my cheek, her warmth filling me and bringing me back to my true self.

Waking back on the couch, I wiped my cheeks clean. Jenks purred at my side, his little paw outstretched and resting atop my heart. "Thank you, sweet boy. I know you miss her too."

The fire flared, and I laughed out loud. This home… this life we'd created here was ingrained in me, and while I did love Roarke, I didn't need his magic to be happy. I only needed him.

By early evening, I'd cast five more spells trying to identify Agitha or her bloodline in any way.

"Dammit." I tossed my pendulum down onto my altar cloth, failing yet again. It was as though the information was somehow being blocked from me. "I'm running out of ideas, buddy. Got any suggestions?"

Jenks lowered himself to the ground, covering his head with his front paws.

"It's okay, baby. I'll figure it out." I didn't want him to feel like he was letting me down, but the truth was I had no idea what to do next. My only option was to meet Roarke in the dreamscape and tell him what was going on.

Maybe if he accepted my plan to break the curse, he could help me identify where to go and who I needed to find. But the idea of telling him I was walking away made my stomach churn and my heart ache.

If we lived in a perfect world, I wouldn't have to choose at all. I could continue to be Roarke's queen in and out of the dreamscape without harming anyone along the way.

I thought back to my day spent with Mama and imagined staying there forever, embracing my dreams and the ones I loved.

I had no doubt others felt the same way. If given the choice, to escape the hardships of life and live within your dreams would be anyone's preference. But that was it, wasn't it? The Weavers couldn't allow that choice.

Without nightmares, people would lose themselves in the fantasy of their peaceful dreams, becoming completely removed from the world. Nightmares were the dose of reality everyone needed to stay safe. Warnings your subconscious offered as a way to prepare you for life. It was like raising a child. If they weren't taught to fear the fire, they would walk straight into it. Or play with a spider or snake that could kill them, if their parents hadn't faced that fear of their own and taught them to steer clear of such things.

The Queen of Nightmares was a necessity to bring balance to the masses, but it was a role I wasn't cut out for and simply couldn't keep. Mama was right. I knew who I was deep within my soul.

I would face Roarke tonight and relinquish his magic, but not before he knew how much I loved him and that what I was doing was for the good of us both.

I would make sure we could be together in the end. That was the truth of who I was. I knew what I wanted, and I would never stop until my dream came true.

Focused and ready, I crawled into bed, discarding my crystals and petting Jenks one more time. "I'll be back soon, sweet boy, but stay close and get some rest."

Jenks nuzzled into my side, curling up into a ball. With his rhythmic purring vibrating against me, it didn't take long for me to fall asleep.

"Milly, my god, are you all right?" Roarke's panicked voice pulled me roughly into the dreamscape, waking me outside his cabin as he gripped my shoulders in strong, shaking hands. "I've been so worried about you."

I stretched onto my tiptoes and placed a kiss on his lips, then moved out of his embrace. "I'm fine. I just needed time to work some things out." I veered off the path, walking toward the edge of the island instead. I didn't want to be inside his cabin when I told him the truth in case I needed to force myself to leave.

"But the gate!" he exclaimed, causing my heart to race.

"Was there another attack?" I thought my spell had held Isabelle in place, but Roarke's frantic eyes had me doubting my strength again.

"No. Thankfully not. But you said you wouldn't leave me alone again, especially with the gate at risk." He ran a hand through his hair, pulling the short tresses into a wild, spiky mess.

This wasn't about the gate. His fear was about being alone.

I reached out and squeezed his hand, attempting to calm him in the smallest way. "Will you walk with me?"

We ventured to the familiar bank in silence, the serene landscape pulling at my soul. I needed to commit the snow peaks to memory, etching the hidden home of my beloved into my mind before breaking his heart.

"Can we sit?" I asked, waiting as he lowered himself to the ground.

I joined him, dipping my toes into the frigid water of the surrounding mountain lake. With a simple thought and a smile on my face, I used my Weaver magic one last time to bring the water up to a tolerable temperature. "There. That's better."

Roarke watched me closely, his eyes full of worry. "Milly, what's going on? I can tell there's something wrong."

My chin quivered, my attempt to be brave threatening to collapse at his genuine concern. "There are so many things I need to tell you. Things I've recently learned that will affect us both."

"Milly, please. Let me know what's bothering you so I can make it right."

The heartbreak in his voice told me he thought this was about him. And though he was right in a way, I quickly set his mind at ease.

"Roarke, you've done nothing wrong. But this isn't something you can help me with." I scooted closer, leaning my head against his shoulder. "In fact, it's something *I* have to do to help *you*."

He kissed the top of my head. "What do you mean? Are you talking about the gate?"

The water of the lake shimmered in the distance, and I allowed myself another moment to take it all in. Lifting my head, I kissed Roarke soundly on the lips, despair already knotting in my throat.

"I need you to listen, okay? The rules about your magic are all a lie. Your bloodline was cursed a long time ago, but I'm going to make things right." I reached out, needing to feel him beneath my hands.

He pulled away.

"What are you talking about?" He pushed to his feet. "You don't know anything about my bloodline." He gestured to the water and the pristine snowcapped mountains surrounding us. "And how could any of this be a curse?"

He snapped his fingers, and a moment later, we were back in Greece. Then Venice at sunset. Another snap and my favorite English garden appeared.

"Milly, there's no way my magic is a curse."

I sighed, seeing this was going to be even harder than I thought.

"It's not your magic that's cursed, Roarke. It's you and your entire family line." I grabbed his arm as he turned to walk away. "A witch named Agitha cursed one of the original Weavers a long time ago because he didn't choose her as his queen. Ever since then, the 'rules' of only interacting in the dreamscape have been a result of that curse. She damned your line to live a half life, but I promise, I'm going to make this right."

Roarke stared at me, his eyes growing dark. "If the Weaver line is such a curse, I guess you no longer want to be my queen. Is that why you were gone last night? Is that what you needed to *work out?*"

He stomped out of the greenhouse, crushing a rose in his hand as he walked away.

"Roarke, wait! I need to finish explaining so you'll understand."

He spun around, fury and pain written across his face. "Oh, I understand. You realized your magic was the opposite of mine and decided you're too good to be my queen. Too innocent and unwilling to acknowledge the world as it truly is."

"No!" I shook my head, wounded by his words, but I forced myself to rush on. "Well, yes, but it's not like that. I do have a problem inflicting nightmares upon the world, but what I'm trying to explain is that the magic doesn't matter! Being your queen doesn't matter! I only want you!" I raced forward, desperate for him to see my side of things. "I have to walk away from the Weaver magic, but only because I want to break the curse so we can be together for real." I grabbed his arms. "Roarke, I love you. Please let me do this for you. For us."

Tears swirled in his eyes, mixing with shadows and turning them into a deep dark pool. "I love you too." His voice felt like gravel against my skin. "But if you do this, I'll be forced to choose another queen. And you will never see me again. If you relinquish your magic, your dreams will be like everyone else's, and there will be nothing I can do."

I sobbed, hating every word that slipped past his lips, but in my gut, I knew I could do this.

"I promise I can make this right. Choose your next queen, but know I'll never stop fighting to break you free of this life." I raced into his arms to kiss him one last time.

Roarke's body quaked as we held each other tight—our hearts breaking in unison. His soft cries only caused my sobs to grow louder, the heartache of what I needed to do completely overwhelming us both.

He placed kiss after kiss atop my head, refusing to let me go. But finally, I forced myself to pull away.

Peering into his watery eyes, I took in every curve and crevice, etching everything about him deeper into my soul. "I'll never stop fighting to find my way back to you, but I have to do this."

With tears streaming down his cheeks, Roarke gripped my hand, and the magic between us flared in my palm, seeping from my veins back into his own with nothing more than a thought.

I crushed my mouth to his, lingering as long as I could before he was pulled back to the gate. It was then that my heart truly broke.

I dropped to the ground, knowing without a doubt who would be waiting for him there.

Isabelle had already marked it with her own magic, forcing the Weaver to see her as his only choice. It sickened me, but I refused to let it derail my plans. I had a mission of my own, and nothing would stop me from achieving my goal. Roarke and I *would* be together in the real world, and I wouldn't quit until we were both free from this curse. But for now, I lay still, cocooned in my sorrow as my endless tears soaked the soft grass beneath me, marring my favorite place.

29

Three months later...

MILKWEED, NETTLE, AND THORNS FROM MY blackberry bush sat crushed in my mortar. The contents would fill my witch bottles, replenishing the protections around my home.

The moment Isabelle had become queen, my nightmares erupted in full force. Tortured visions of myself or Roarke being beaten and punished within the depths of hell was a favorite of hers. And despite knowing it was all a dream, I woke nightly, my throat raw from screaming.

With my ingredients prepared, I poured them into four jars, along with shards of glass, stick pins, and a snippet of my hair, covering it all in red wine.

Sealing the lids, I pulled on my boots and coat, then walked to each corner of my house. With the quick work of the shovel, I buried a jar beneath the snow in each direction. It might not stop her from torturing me in the dreamscape, but at least it would help protect me and Jenks from anything she might choose to will into the real world.

Besides in my nightmares, I hadn't seen Roarke since walking away, and his words haunted me more than anything else. *"If you do this, I'll be forced to choose another queen. And you will never see me again. If you relinquish your magic, your dreams will be like everyone else's, and there will be nothing I can do."*

Tomorrow was the first day since my last encounter with Isabelle that I'd be traveling outside of Rhode Island. I needed to follow up on a clue I'd found buried in a tattered manuscript I uncovered at the library in the next town over. It wasn't a smoking gun by any means, but there were mentions of a witch named Agitha traveling through the surrounding region, so I had to give it a shot. Keelyn continued to let me borrow her car as long as I continued to deliver fresh ingredients and cook her a meal or two every now and again.

Pulling my coat tight, I fought the wind as I headed back inside. Winter was in full swing, and while I usually enjoyed this time of year, I couldn't help but notice its exaggerated effects on me. My body felt weaker than it ever had before, and even the warmest fire couldn't chase the chill from my bones.

Wrapped in my afghan, I reviewed my plotted course. I would be traveling to Hartford, Connecticut, a place I'd never been before, but the librarian I spoke with there said she had a variety of old newspaper clippings and brochures from around the same time as the book I had discovered. She agreed to have them prepared and laid out for me when I arrived, so all in all, the trip shouldn't take me long.

I had never spent the night in a hotel or taken a vacation of any kind, even when Mama was alive. If she ever did have to venture away from home, she was only gone for the day, selling our wares or trading for new crystals and tools. And any farmers markets we visited in the nearby towns were close enough we were able to return home each night, the structured habit growing comfortable over my younger years. With my track record of what happened in Maine with Isabelle, I wasn't exactly looking forward to leaving my home, but I couldn't let Roarke down. I would search to the ends of the earth to find the answers we needed.

With the fire stoked, I finished the last of my chamomile tea and climbed into bed. "I would ask you to join me, sweet boy, but I'm afraid I might hurt you with all my tossing and turning." I petted Jenks on the head and lowered him to the floor, signaling he should sleep in his own bed instead.

Tucking a piece of amethyst, black tourmaline, moonstone, and pink calcite beneath my pillow, I lay down and closed my eyes. Isabelle had broken through every ritual I previously tried, but hopefully, tonight would be different—though somehow I knew the nightmares would come all the same.

Roarke's screams lingered in my ears even after I woke. The chilling scene had taken on a familiar tone until an anaconda the size of a twenty-foot tree wrapped itself around me, keeping my dream self from helping while Roarke was skinned alive.

I wondered if he knew how Isabelle was torturing me or if she'd taken over the dreamscape so completely that he couldn't do anything about it even if he wanted to.

I tried not to think about them working side by side every night. The images my mind conjured brought their own set of nightmares that I couldn't possibly face.

My mind and body yearned to reconnect with Roarke even as I continued to feel less and less like myself.

Forcing down a light breakfast of toast and tea, I gathered my map and notes and bundled up in my boots and coat. Stumbling along the path, I meandered through the woods, my restless nights getting the better of me as I headed to the library to retrieve Keelyn's car.

Hartford was approximately seventy miles away, and it should only take about an hour and a half to get there. I smiled, happy I'd be able to return home again tonight.

"Morning—" Keelyn began but startled when she met my eyes. "Honey… are you okay? You look like death on a cracker."

"Gee, thanks." I slid into a nearby chair, my legs barely able to keep me upright after my hike through the woods. "I haven't been sleeping well."

"I can tell. Are you sure you're going to be okay to run your errands today? It's not about the car…" She rushed on. "But you don't exactly look alert enough to drive."

My eyes drooped just as I heard her say, "Let me get you some coffee."

A scream pulled me upright, and Keelyn was there, shaking my shoulders.

"My god, Milly. What is going on? You fell asleep in the chair, and the next thing I knew, you were screaming like a banshee."

I looked around the library, thankful no one else had entered yet this morning. "I'm so sorry. How embarrassing." I took the coffee she offered, its bitter, unfamiliar taste a shock to my system. "Thank you."

"Of course. Now why don't you come with me to the back office and lie down for a bit?"

"I can't. I have a meeting in Hartford I don't want to miss."

Keelyn looked around the library, noting it was still just the two of us inside. "Then how about this… I'll close the library for the day and drive you myself instead. Will that work?"

My head dipped, sleep ready to pull me under again. "Yes. Thank you. That would be great."

I gave Keelyn my directions, then let her lead me to the car, settling into the passenger seat. I fell back asleep before we even reached the edge of town. Another of Isabelle's nightmares gripped me, but it wasn't as intense during the day.

I woke with Keelyn shaking me again, genuine concern painted across her face. "Milly, what's going on? I've never known you to have night terrors before. Did something happen that you want to talk about?"

I contemplated telling her everything but knew I couldn't. This disaster was mine and mine alone. "No. Nothing specific. Like I said, I just haven't been sleeping well, so when I do, I guess my mind gets a little crazy." I shrugged, hoping she bought the lie.

"Well, you need to figure out how to get some sleep, sweetie, because this isn't healthy."

Tell me about it.

"I know. Just last night, I mixed a fresh batch of chamomile tea, so I'll be fine soon. Don't worry."

Keelyn stared at me, her ice-blue eyes penetrating mine as if she could see all the way into my soul. "Milly, since the day your mother died, all I've done is worry about you. I thought you'd know that by now."

I turned back to the window, thankful yet sad.

The rest of the drive was a blur of fresh landscapes and old buildings I'd never seen before. The snow-covered hills, evergreens and oaks, and brick structures were familiar enough, but I had to admit it was nice to experience someplace new.

Keelyn pulled up to the curb outside the Connecticut State Library and cut the engine. "If you're sure you'll be okay, I'm going to do some shopping while you attend your meeting. I'll be back by one if that works for you."

I gathered my bag containing my notes and climbed out of the car. "That'll be perfect. And, Keelyn, thank you again... for everything."

With a smile and a little wave, Keelyn drove off, leaving me to climb the concrete stairs up to the two-story building.

The Hartford library reminded me of the White House or a plantation-type mansion with its white plaster exterior and four large Roman-style columns framing three front doors. Above each wood entrance were large curved windows crosshatched with black muntins, giving the overall classic design a slightly modern twist.

Entering through the center door, I approached the help desk and asked for Ms. Dutton.

"Milly Atwood?" the receptionist asked.

I nodded.

"She's got you all set up in meeting room number four. You'll find her just up those stairs." She pointed to her left with a friendly smile on her face.

"Thank you."

I climbed the stairs, finding Ms. Dutton waiting for me, her wrinkled hands clasped in front of her knee-length beige skirt. Papers of all sorts and sizes were spread out on a long conference room table, arranged chronologically from what I could tell.

"Ms. Atwood, it's nice to meet you. I was so intrigued by your inquiry that I might have gone a little overboard in my own research." Ms. Dutton laughed, her three-quarter reading glasses sliding precariously down her hawklike nose.

"Well, I'm certainly impressed. Thank you very much."

"You're more than welcome to take pictures, but I'll have to ask that you don't remove any of the documents from this room. They'll be transferred back to the archives once you finish with them today."

I looked over the sea of paper, praying at least one sliver of the parchment would hold another clue.

"I promise I won't."

30

TWO AND A HALF HOURS LATER, PILES of paper now littered the table, sectioned into stacks of what I deemed relevant or not—the *relevant* stack being the smallest of them all.

I'd read about the history of the colonies and the witch hunts that occurred up and down the East Coast, but none of the articles mentioned Agitha by name. The only clues I found mentioned a string of nightmares terrorizing the local children in 1602 until one day they miraculously stopped.

I wasn't sure if that tied into the Weaver's magic or if Agitha and her curse were somehow involved. But it was the only thing I found that sounded faintly familiar, so I pulled the thread, taking notes and reading as much as I could before my time here was up.

The strange outbreak ended up being labeled a mass delusion brought on by bad water gathered from a tainted creek. The officials at the time deemed it illegal to gather anything else from the local source, their warning and imposed rules *saving* the town.

I shook my head, imagining how easily this could have been manipulated by a witch. My thoughts drifted to Isabelle and my recurring nightmares, and I wondered if that, too, was her intent. To force me to go crazy, my mind and body completely shutting down.

The door to the meeting room opened, and Ms. Dutton walked inside. "Did you find what you were looking for, dear?"

I stared back at the pitiful piles and shook my head. "Not conclusively, but thank you for all your hard work and help. I never would have gotten this far if you hadn't pulled all these articles in advance. I truly appreciate it."

The old librarian smiled. "It was no problem in the slightest. All part of my job."

Part of my job, I thought.

It was the Queen of Nightmares' job to bring balance to the Weaver's magic, not overshadow it. I was more desperate than ever to reach Roarke and see if he was okay.

Thanking Ms. Dutton again, I gathered my things and raced downstairs, fleeing the library when I spotted Keelyn's car waiting out front.

I slammed into the passenger seat, chilled from the cold but also in a rush to get home. "Let's go."

Keelyn chuckled. "Gee, okay. Nice to see you've woken up and are functioning again in the land of the living."

"Sorry, yeah. I think my catnap on the way here was just what I needed."

"Well, good." Keelyn veered onto the main road that would lead us back out of town. "So how did your meeting go? Did you find what you came looking for?"

"Not exactly, but I have an idea of what I need to do next."

"Does this have anything to do with the book you bought from me?"

I hadn't mentioned the book, so I wasn't sure why she was asking. But I didn't think it would hurt to discuss my dilemma in a vague sort of way.

"Partly, I guess. There was a person referenced in the book that I'm trying to track down, but I haven't found any other text or articles that explain who she was or where her family originated from."

"What's her name? Maybe I can do another search for you and see what I can find."

I hesitated, my nerves twisting in my gut. "It's okay. I've actually exhausted all the library's material and didn't find anything of use. But like I said, I think I know what to do next."

"And what's that?"

I looked out the window, not sure how to explain or even that I could. "There's one person who may be able to help, but I've been having trouble reaching them. I should know tonight, though, whether my plan will work or not."

"Well, keep me posted. If there's anything you need, just let me know."

"Thanks, Keelyn. I will."

Actually, I wouldn't, but she didn't need to know that.

"Sweetie, we're here." Keelyn's voice and the light pressure of her hand against my shoulder pulled me back from the edge of sleep.

I looked out the window, grateful to see we'd returned home. "Thank you for the ride. I'm sorry my exhaustion caused you to close the library."

Keelyn smiled. "I should be thanking you. Today was like a mini vacation." She laughed. "But are you sure you're okay? You don't look so good, and I've never seen you so... drained."

I took a deep breath and shook my head, forcing myself awake. "It's been awhile since I've taken a road trip. I guess the lull of the car can still put me to sleep."

Her eyes narrowed at my lame excuse.

"Thanks again." Before she could question me further, I exited the car and shuffled to my front door.

Keelyn waved out the window. "Get some sleep, Milly, and I hope things work out the way you want."

Me too.

I lifted a hand goodbye, then rushed into the house, stepping over Jenks as he raced to greet me. "Come on, sweet boy. I'm going to need your help."

Setting up my altar, I unpinned the memory circle from above my bed and laid it next to my gathered ingredients. My hope was to connect with Roarke's energy ingrained in the treasures he'd willed through the dreamscape for me, providing a link directly to him.

If I was able to bypass Isabelle completely, hopefully, I could check on Roarke without her even knowing I was there.

Plucking the flowers from the woven twine, I held them in my left hand and slipped the circle over my right.

Connected through our future's past, bring me safely to him at last. Cutting through the nightmare within, allow me to see my lover again.

A deep scream rent the air, the Weaver's Gate flickering in the distance. Roarke's body lay collapsed on the ground, leaning against the outside of the mountain. I ran toward him as fast as I could, my feet pounding the hard earth like a herd of gazelle fleeing a predator.

Falling to my knees, I pushed back the hood of his cloak. "My god, what is she doing to you?"

Roarke's lids fluttered open, his eyes nothing more than glossed-over gray pools.

Thunder boomed overhead, angry and loud as if Mamu and Zaqu were trying to beat their way back onto this plane.

Roarke's prone body was limp and lethargic, but at least he was still alive.

I slipped my arm under his, trying to heave him off the ground. "Come on, please," I begged the gods. "Give me the strength."

I thought if I could get him inside the gate, perhaps a fresh boost of their Weaver magic could break whatever spell was affecting him.

I limped closer to the open door, pulling him along the best I could.

Rays of cosmic light still poured through the top of the mountain, culminating in a pure beam of magical energy straight from the gods. Sparks flew from the concentrated beam, sending shards of stars colliding into our world.

I pulled the hood of Roarke's cloak over his head, his previous words ringing loudly in my mind. *"Only Weavers are allowed inside. And it's important you understand that. Anyone not chosen who enters the gate would be destroyed instantly. Even with our cloaks in place for protection, the energy is beyond anything in this world."*

I considered taking the cloak for myself to give me the best chance of survival, but in his current state, Roarke needed all the protection he could get. Besides, without being chosen to enter, it probably wouldn't matter anyway. I would most likely be destroyed the second I stepped inside. But I didn't care as long as I could save him.

With every ounce of strength I had left, I dragged him through the open door of the mountain and thrust him into the gate.

Screaming at the top of my lungs, I woke in my bed. Jenks hissed from the floor and arched his back, growling at the shadow in the corner of my room.

"Did you really think it would be that easy? That you could show up in the dreamscape without me knowing?" Isabelle's voice cracked with disdain.

It had all been another nightmare.

"Roarke is fine by the way. But you'll never reach him again."
She stepped out of the dark, her eyes still the same sickly yellow-green as the last time I saw her. "I will torture you forever if you don't give up this silly quest."

Ah! So that's what all this was about. She knew I was trying to break the curse.

I tossed back my blankets with dramatic flair and crossed the room. She might have tricked her way into the Weaver's magic, but I had no doubt I was the stronger witch.

"The fact that you're here only proves how nervous you are that I'll succeed." I shoved a finger in her face. "And have no doubt... I *will.*"

Jenks prowled behind me, walking in circles atop the sigil I'd traced beneath the rug.

"Now be gone!" I threw out my hand, Jenks pouncing straight up and down in the same instant. A flare of pure silver light blasted through the room, activating my spell. The sigil glowed brightly, banishing every shadow in my house and Isabelle along with them.

"Good job, sweet boy. You're my hero."

I knew at some point Isabelle would use her stolen magic to break my wards and come here, but I was ready. Now I just had to find a way to truly reach Roarke, and her latest nightmare had given me the perfect idea.

31

IF ISABELLE HAD GAINED ACCESS TO THE gate from the real world, then so could I.

Roarke had chosen me as his true queen, so if I could erase Isabelle's tainted magic from the source, perhaps I could get rid of her and sever her connection as the impostor she was.

Doing this would alter my plans to break the curse, but Isabelle was becoming a curse all her own. And despite if she was telling the truth and Roarke was truly okay, I couldn't keep living like this. At least this way I could bring us both some peace, if only from afar.

I double-checked the wards around my house, making sure Isabelle was truly gone. Gathering my little black book, I flipped to the pages where the history of the Weaver's magic was discussed. Genevieve hadn't mentioned the gate by name or laid out who the gods were from which the magic originated. But judging by how she discussed the topic, she definitely must have known. I imagined Isabelle's copy of the book having annotations written in the margins, leaving me with even less information than I thought.

As much as I wanted to help Roarke—and myself—in reality, I had no idea how to break into a god-made magical gate, let alone undo whatever corruption Isabelle had achieved.

I sank down onto the living room floor, welcoming Jenks into my lap. "I don't know what to do, buddy. I just keep hitting nothing but dead ends." I buried my face in his fur and let the tears come full force.

It had been three months since I walked away, and everything I'd tried so far had ended in failure. The way things were going, it could easily be years before I figured out a way to see Roarke again. And with my strength continuing to wane, soon I probably wouldn't be able to do any magic at all—giving Isabelle exactly what she wanted.

A gust blew down the chimney, sending sparks flying into the room just as a knock sounded at the door.

With my heart lodged in my throat, I crept to the front windows, peering out into the dark.

A group of huddled shadows stood just beyond my gate, seemingly waiting for a signal from the one standing on my stoop.

"Who's there?" I cried, panicked and scared. Never before had I felt this vulnerable or alone.

"Milly, it's Keelyn. Open up, sweetie."

I eased the door open, sucking in a shocked breath.

Keelyn stood in front of me with a cloak around her shoulders and twelve women wearing the same thing waiting at her back. "I figured it was time I brought my 'book club' to you." She winked, her ice-blue eyes sparkling like diamonds. "Now move aside and let us old witches help nurse you back to health."

Keelyn's group streamed through my door and into the living room, spreading out their tools and herbs across my floor.

"I don't understand," I sobbed, grateful to see her familiar face even in this unfamiliar way.

My longtime friend pulled me into the kitchen, away from the rest of the women. "Milly, Josephine might have been a solitary witch, but she was also my friend. And she asked me a long time ago if I would keep an eye on you."

I sank into the rickety chair, hobbled by the mention of my mother's name.

"She asked that I keep my practices to myself, knowing you'd need to find your own way. But she did leave me this." Keelyn pulled out a moonstone the size of a small boulder, and all thoughts raced from my head. "She said that if it were to ever start glowing like this, it meant you were in trouble and your magic was at risk. Only then did she want me to intervene." She placed the stone in my hand, reaching into her cloak to retrieve something else.

"And if that time did ever come, she also wanted you to have this." Keelyn handed me a small, hand-bound book, its edges crunched and crinkled from the wear of time. "She wanted you to know the truth, Milly, but would never force her decisions upon you."

I stared at the precious objects in my hand, no longer processing Keelyn's words. All thoughts flew from my head as I stared at my friend, tracing back through all the years we'd known each other. She'd been my mom's friend first—a witch tasked with protecting me—and I didn't have a clue. I shook my head, still struggling for words as I looked down at the magical gifts she'd brought me. Magical gifts my mother had given her. But why?

I gently flipped open the first page of the book, crying in earnest as I stared at my mother's handwriting.

My Dearest Milly,

Forgive my methods, but you needed to walk this path on your own. If you're reading this now, it means you've learned of the Weaver's existence and your role as his queen. It is an honored tradition bestowed upon the Atwood women from the beginning of time. Not only was the Weaver's bloodline chosen by the gods but so were their queens.

The choice, however, remains your own to accept and to walk with the power, knowing what it will do. Or you can walk away from the magic forever. If you're reading this now, I already know the choice you made.

As hard as it was, I, too, walked away, choosing to live a normal life with your father instead, and I wouldn't have had it any other way.

For a witch to lose her magic is never easy, but Keelyn will guide you back to health just as she did me. You, my darling Milly, were the greatest joy of my life, and I hope you will find peace in this happiness too. If, however, you want to return, I have one more gift for you.

I turned the page, revealing a small stick resting in the seam.

This is the last remaining shard from the wand of Agitha Atwood.

Scorned by a weaver when he chose her sister instead, Agitha cursed their line throughout time, but with this, you can set things right if that's what you choose.

I can't imagine all you've gone through since I've been gone, but know that if you follow your heart, your head will find a way.

Trust yourself, Milly, and know I believe in you. I love you so much, and all I want is for you to be happy.

As I stared at the brittle pages, my tears threatened to ruin the dark-blue ink. Though there was more to read, I closed the book, learning all I needed to know for now.

Keelyn cleared her throat, bringing me back to myself. "Milly, if you're ready and willing, we can stop the drain on your magic."

I thought back to all the time Mom and I had spent together in the garden—me using my magic to nurture the soil and plants and Mama always eager to share her lessons with me. But all the while, I never once saw her use actual magic herself.

"She chose to give it all away?" I wiped my cheeks with the back of my hand.

Keelyn knelt in front of me. "Yes, sweetie, she did. And not because of any curse or because she wasn't a powerful witch but because she knew her own heart and wanted nothing more than to raise a family with your dad."

I thought about what that meant and the timeline of it all. If the Atwoods were the Weavers' designated queens, that meant at least three of my ancestors could have possibly been Roarke's. He'd been the Weaver for a hundred and seventy-five years and never once found his partner... until me.

I wondered if he met my mom and she chose to walk away or if she made her choice before she ever saw him in her dreams. From the tone of her words in the book, it seemed I was the first Atwood who'd been kept in the dark. But that was okay. I forgave her.

I turned to Keelyn. "What do I have to do to get my magic back?"

I still wasn't interested in being Roarke's Queen of Nightmares, but I needed access to my inherent magic if I was going to face Isabelle and break this damn curse once and for all.

32

RHYTHMIC CHANTS AND DRUMS FILLED MY cottage as the West Greenwich coven focused all their energy solely on me. Jenks lay atop my stomach, providing a grounding tether as they worked their magic, each taking on a different role.

Keelyn knelt behind me, my head resting in her lap, while six other women—three on each side—held their hands above the crystals lining my arms and legs. The other six ladies walked in a circle beyond that, pounding their drums and spinning their magic.

For a solitary witch, this was something!

"Just relax, Milly. Close your eyes. Focus and center. Locate the source of your power."

I followed Keelyn's instructions, feeling a pulse buried deep within my stomach.

The drums and chants grew louder, but I kept my eyes closed. A swell of magic emerged inside me, unfurling and growing like the plants I'd tended in our garden. I always knew my magic was part of the land.

Keelyn had explained that Mama didn't want her magic back, only to be healthy enough to live a normal life with me and my dad.

It made me feel selfish for a moment, as though I was asking for too much, but as my magic unfolded and reached my heart, I knew I'd made the right decision.

I recalled my words to Roarke, their truth meaning more to me now than ever. *"The magic doesn't matter! Being your queen doesn't matter! I only want you!"*

I understood the choice Mama made, but it wasn't the right choice for me. I needed my magic if I was going to break this curse, and doing so was the first step toward the life I envisioned with Roarke.

"Hold still just a few more moments," Keelyn whispered in my ear as Jenks let out a loud, commanding yowl.

I lifted my head, unable to form words. Mr. Jenkins's black fur was now covered in gold symbols. Vines, flowers, and leaves marked his body while a crescent moon sat squarely above his bright amber eyes.

"What's this about?" I asked, running a hand down my familiar's back.

"He wanted to help," Keelyn said, maneuvering out from under me. "This will protect your magic for the rest of his—and *your*—exceptionally long life."

Sitting cross-legged in the middle of my room, I placed my forehead against Mr. Jenkins. "Always my hero."

Atwood familiars could live hundreds of years, and I knew Jenks's choice to link our magic further was meant to give me as much time with Roarke in the real world as he could. My sweet boy had always been there since the day I was born, passed down from Mama to me, and always aware of all of our needs.

"Thank you, baby. I'll never forget what you've done." I lifted my head, repeating my words to the room. "I'll never forget what any of you have done." I stood and threw myself into Keelyn's arms. "Thank you all so much."

The coven members quietly gathered their things, patting me on the back as they departed my home, leaving Keelyn and me alone.

She pulled back from our hug. "So you're not mad at me for keeping your mom's secret?"

I pushed her long silver-blond braid over her shoulder, reveling in the fact that she was actually a witch too. "No, I'm not mad. As a matter of fact, I've never been happier. Though, I do have one more question."

"What's that?"

"Do you know if my mother knew Genevieve DuWant—or Genevieve Pike?" I didn't want to think of Mama as her source, but that was one mystery I still hadn't solved. "If not her, maybe my grandmother?"

"Not that I know of. Besides me and a few women in town, your mother didn't have many friends. All she ever needed was your father and you."

I grinned, wiping another happy tear from my cheek and resolved to the fact that I might never know.

"It's good to see you smile, Milly. But I assume there's one person who can make you even happier than this."

I laughed, realizing she already knew I was in love with Roarke.

"I love him so much. And now, with your and Mama's help, I can break this damn curse so we can live out our lives together."

Keelyn smiled, but her eyes remained tight. "Just don't rush into anything too quickly. You need time to recover and for your magic to recharge." She gathered her remaining things and walked to the door. "Promise me you'll rest for a few days at least, okay?" She ran a motherly hand down my arm, leaving me to shout my promise out the door into the night.

"I promise, and thanks again."

Two weeks later...

With my magic restored, I was finally able to block Isabelle and get a good night's sleep. Jenks purred beside me as dawn slowly broke in the sky. The ritual had put a strain on him as well. White beams from the winter sun streamed through the windows, casting new hope on my darkest days.

For the past two weeks, I'd attempted to break into the dreamscape, ready to end Roarke's curse. But just as I'd been able to block Isabelle here in the real world, she'd been able to block me there. But today, as I lay in bed with Mama's notebook clutched in my hands, I finally knew what I had to do. She and Keelyn had been right. I needed to give my body time enough to recover, and after so many failed attempts, it was also time to use my heart *and* my head.

I had no idea walking away from the Weaver's magic meant I was relinquishing my own, and I was sure Roarke didn't know either. To be honest, I thought it was just another side effect of what Isabelle had done to me. But once again, thanks to Mama's foresight, Keelyn's intervention had literally saved my life.

After reading the rest of Mama's notes about how the Atwoods, too, had been chosen by the gods, it became clear that with Agitha's shard, I should be able to enter the gate itself.

Easing from bed, I pulled on my winter robe and rushed to stoke the fire. Testing my magic, I flicked my wrist at the hearth and smiled when the flames burst back to life.

After a hearty breakfast of bacon, oatmeal, toast, and tea, I showered, dressed, and gathered my things.

Laying out a black altar cloth on the dining room table, I spread out my tools—my regular altar too small to fit everything I'd need.

I marked each direction with candles of green, red, yellow, and blue, then rang a bell, activating each one.

Guardians of the north, south, east, and west, bless this house and this quest. Protect me from any who seek to do harm, guarded by my familiar to sound the alarm.

Jenks meowed from beneath the table, curled up and ready to do his part.

Lighting my smudge stick, I used the eagle feather I'd foraged from the woods last spring to wave the smoke into a circle around the space.

Alight upon your sacred wing. Carry the air as it clings. Protect this space and hide me well. Blessed by the gods, we seal this spell.

A ring of smoke hung in the air, encircling the table at chest height.

Sprinkling salt into the black bowl, I filled it with water, then pricked my thumb with my athame. Three drops of blood dripped into the bowl, and I waited for the surface to calm. As the ripples settled, I pressed my hand to the picture of the Weaver's Gate I'd drawn, holding the remnant of Agitha's wand tightly in my other hand.

I peered into the dark surface of the scrying bowl.

God and Goddess, allow me to see, the access being hidden from me. Grant me a boon, from above, to save the one that I do love.

The water rippled in the bowl, a tiny pinprick of light forming at the bottom. Squinting, I leaned in closer for a better look.

Spreading through the water, the light continued to grow, filling the black bowl with a silver energy I'd only felt once before.

A beam so bright I had to shield my eyes shot out of the vessel, piercing my ceiling and continuing straight into the sky.

I looked back to the bowl, noticing movement in the bottom again. A dark square formed at the base of the light, and I gasped. I was looking out the door from *inside* the Weaver's Gate to the barren landscape beyond—where Isabelle stood alone.

Pulling up the hood of the white cloak my mother gifted me when I first accepted my magic, I closed my eyes and pressed my face into the beam of light. It was time to bring this to an end.

Transported, my feet touched solid ground as a warm sensation bloomed around me.

Slowly, tentatively, I opened my eyes.

I was standing inside the gate, the cosmos flooding in from above, pouring the gods' power straight into my soul. I looked out the open door, noticing Isabelle racing toward me as fast as she could. Dark, lightning-streaked clouds lined the sky behind her, their angry red tint transforming the landscape into her personal realm of nightmares. Without warning, she flung out her hand, lightning zinging past my head, as she raced toward the gate.

Chunks of mountain rained down upon me, forcing me to take cover behind the pedestal in the center of the room.

"Milly, I have to give you credit. Coming here was incredibly brave but also incredibly stupid," Isabelle taunted over the chaos outside. "You will never stop me. You're just as weak and useless as ever," she screamed, vitriol spewing from her lips as more lightning crashed around me.

Peeking around from my hidden position, tears welled in my eyes as I watched her creep closer to the mountain's base. Yes, my magic was back, but her words sliced through any bravery I'd conjured up to come here, leaving me raw and terrified.

I raised a shaking hand, sending out a blast of power to stop her, but she just kept coming. A vicious wind stirred up debris behind her, pulling lightning and sand into a glass-pierced tornado that followed in her wake.

Ducking back behind the podium, I pulled my knees to my chest, curling into a ball and crying in earnest. Everything I tried and planned for was all for nothing. Breaking the curse. Saving Roarke... None of it would happen, and it was all because of me. All because Isabelle was right. I was never strong enough to be his queen.

"Time to say goodbye, Milly. You don't belong here anymore."

Wiping my cheeks, I peered around the pedestal, looking back to see how close she was. I froze, meeting her sickly eyes as she stood just outside the door.

A sinister laugh filled the cavern, and a vicious smile spread across her face as Roarke appeared beside her.

I gasped. He was just as beautiful as I remembered but seemed... *smaller* somehow. Drained of power and sadder than I'd ever seen him before. He looked up, processing the scene, his dull eyes going wide when they finally landed on me.

He recoiled from Isabelle, but she caught his arm, violently shocking him and holding him in place.

"Let go of me!" he screamed.

Isabelle's taunting laughter filled the night sky. "Look at her..." She flung an arm in my direction. "She's burning up in there. I told you she didn't belong here. She was never worthy of your magic."

Roarke struggled against her, his body contorting in pain and still unable to break free.

A fury I'd never felt before rose inside me, scorching me from the inside out. Seeing her hands upon him—his depressed and weakened state—something fractured in me, and a voice filled my head.

"Her magic has tainted the source, breaking our vessel, but you are still true. Accept our gift and bring balance once more."

Tears rolled down my cheeks as the combined voices of Mamu and Zaqu filled my head. Roarke was their broken vessel, and I was the only one who could save him.

Flooded with courage and blessed by the gods, I reached for him, my outstretched hand shimmered with cosmic dust, bubbling and rippling with power. I looked to my other, confirming the shard was still in my grasp, then shouted to the heavens.

Take my magic and combine it with thee. His rightful queen I am meant to be. Balanced as equals from dark to light. Grant us a new role but allow us a life. Broken is the curse my ancestor made. Forgiven and mended on this day. Take my magic and combine it with thee. This is my wish, so mote it be.

The sky erupted above me, flooding the gate with even more power. Lifted off my feet and into the air, I kept my eyes pinned to Roarke's, smiling as they started to glow.

"No!" Isabelle's panicked scream rent the air as pure cosmic light exploded from him, clearing the clouds and disintegrating her essence from the spot upon which she stood. Figments of her body floated into the sky, burned away to ash as he extinguished her tainted presence from this sacred place.

The moment my feet touched the ground, I ran to Roarke.

It was over.

Crashing into him, I buried my head against his chest, his strong arms encircling me and holding me tight. Welcoming me home.

"Milly." My name fell from his lips, whisper-soft and full of longing.

I looked up into his familiar sparkling eyes and gasped—my own reflected back at me, an entire universe held within.

33

Two months later...

I WALKED THROUGH A RIP IN SPACE and into the shadowed forest beyond. The delicate boughs of the evergreen trees still dripped with rain, their familiar scent reminding me of our new home. Reminding me of him.

Tilting my head, I listened for all the hopes and dreams flooding into the dreamscape tonight, weeding through the voices, looking for one.

"It looks like you're tallying the whispers of men."

"Not of men. Only you."

Roarke slid up beside me, taking my hand in his. "The shimmer of the moon tonight reminds me of your eyes." He winked.

I smiled, fully accepting my new role. "But the stars I love and the steps we take are only but a guise," I teased back.

Shooting stars filled the sky, streaking silver against the swirling black, purple, pink, and blue. The Weaver magic was limitless and now fully a part of me. Marked by each other and our blended magic,

I could utilize it the same as Roarke, fully able to do anything I wanted without inflicting nightmares like before. Blessed by the gods, there was no longer light and dark or a balance to maintain. We were only one. The role of the Queen of Nightmares had been destroyed along with Isabelle. Now equals, Roarke and I could live our life together—in the real world *and* in the dreamscape.

He held out my matching cloak and smiled, silver flames dancing in his eyes. "Are you ready to go home?"

I nodded, thinking back to the moment he'd revealed his island to me in the real world.

Surrounded by evergreens and aspens, the tiny cabin looked exactly as it had in the dreamscape. Located on the Loch, this hidden gem was truly secluded on an island buried deep in a mountain pass about three hours outside Estes Park, Colorado. I'd burst into tears when he'd first brought me here. Its beauty and the sense of peace I felt was just as real as it had been in my dreams.

Stepping inside, I bent down and opened my arms, gathering Jenks to my chest as he purred in contentment. "The mountain air seems to suit him."

Roarke kissed my cheek and gave Jenks a scratch behind his ears. "Do you miss it?" he asked, taking a seat on the couch.

"Miss what?"

"Your cottage? Your woods? Your ancestral home? I know it was hard for you to leave your land and your gardens behind."

I joined him on the couch, folding my legs beneath me. "Yes and no. After learning how close Keelyn and my mother were, it felt right to give it to her. I know she'll take good care of it, and I think it's the perfect spot for her and her coven to continue their work."

I snuggled against him, content in my choice. Staring into the flames of the fire, I lost myself in the love we shared and the life we'd built.

Placing a hand on my pregnant belly, Roarke whispered in my ear, "I love you, wife. And you'll *forever* be my queen."

The End

As an added bonus, if you'd like to purchase the non-fiction reference guide to all the plants and herbs Milly used in this book, you can find *Found & Foraged* wherever paperback books are sold.

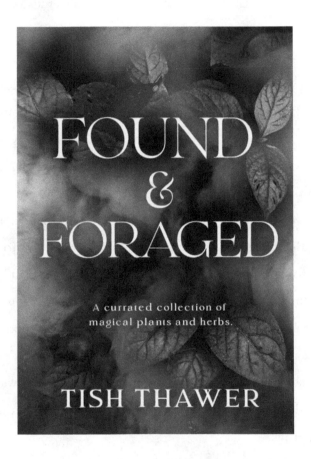

FOUND
&
FORAGED

A currated collection of
magical plants and herbs.

TISH THAWER

(*Found & Foraged* is printed in full color and is a work of non-fiction. All inclusions have been curated and selected from their use in author Tish Thawer's fictional work, *Weaver*. All herbal and medicinal information has been reviewed and verified by herbalists and/or obtained by vetted resources.)

Acknowledgements

To my husband: I don't think I can ever truly express how much I love you and how much your hard work means to me. You truly do make my dreams come true.

To my children: I hope the life we've created for you is something you can look back upon with fondness. (Or at least a little humor and longing the older you get.) I love you with all my heart.

To my best friend, Brynn: Thank you for being my sounding board, my confidant, and the perfect source of joy whenever I need a laugh.

To Cecily, Sharon, Cortney, Stacey, Casey, Cameo, Rebecca, Cambria, Belinda, Laura, Kristie, and Amber: Thank you for reading *Weaver* before publication and providing your feedback and editorial reviews. I'm so grateful to have such amazing friends in this industry.

To my editor, Cassie: Thank you for your consummate professionalism and patience. Your attention to detail and willingness to answer my questions any time of the day was greatly appreciated. You definitely helped me in my efforts to continue to learn and grow.

To all my ARC readers: Thank you for reading *Weaver* early and for your honest feedback and reviews. Your thoughts and suggestions are very much welcomed and appreciated.

And finally, to my readers: "Thank you" doesn't seem like enough to express how grateful I am for all your support. With each book I write, it's my hope to provide another magical escape just for you.

Blessed be,
~ Tish

About the Author

#1 Bestseller in Historical Fiction
Top 100 Bestselling in Paid Kindle Store
Best Cover Award Winner
Readers' Choice Award Winner
Best Sci-fi Fantasy Novel Winner (x2)

Author Tish Thawer writes paranormal romances for all ages. From her first paranormal cartoon, Isis, to the Twilight phenomenon, myth, magic, and superpowers have always held a special place in her heart. Best known for her Witches of BlackBrook series, Tish's detailed world-building and magic-laced stories have been compared to Nora Roberts, Sam Cheever, and Charlaine Harris. Tish's books have been featured in British Glamour and Elle magazines. Tish has worked as a computer consultant, photographer, and graphic designer, and has bylines as a columnist for Gliterary Girl media, RT Magazine, and Literary Lunes Magazine. She currently resides in Missouri with her husband and three wonderful children, and operates Amber Leaf Designs, an online custom swag retail store.

You can find out more about Tish and all her titles by visiting:
www.tishthawer.com

Connect with Tish Thawer Online:
Instagram: @tishthawer
Facebook: www.facebook.com/AuthorTishThawer
Twitter: @tishthawer
Pinterest: www.pinterest.com/tishthawer

If you'd like an email when each new book releases, please sign up for my mailing list. Emails only go out about once per month and your information is closely guarded.
http://www.tishthawer.com/subscribe.html

Also, to get an email for new releases, book updates, and special sales, follow me on BookBub and Goodreads at the links below:
www.bookbub.com/authors/tish-thawer
https://www.goodreads.com/tishthawer

Again, thank you for reading. If you'd like to stay connected and hang out for more magical adventures, you can join my private reader group here:
https://www.facebook.com/groups/TishThawersBookCoven

Also by Tish Thawer

The Witches of BlackBrook
The Witches of BlackBrook - Book 1
The Daughters of Maine - Book 2
The Sisters of Salem – Book 3
Lost in Time – (*A Legends of Havenwood Falls novella,
and a Witches of BlackBrook side-story*)

The Women of Purgatory
Raven's Breath - Book 1
Dark Abigail - Book 2
Holli's Hellfire – Book 3
The Women of Purgatory: The Complete Series bundle

The TS901 Chronicles
TS901: Anomaly – Book 1
TS901: Dominion – Book 2
TS901: Evolution – Book 3

Havenwood Falls Shared World
Lost in Time – (*A Legends of Havenwood Falls novella,
and a Witches of BlackBrook side-story*)
Sun & Moon Academy – Book 1: Fall Semester (*A HWF
Anthology*)
Sun & Moon Academy – Book 2: Spring Semester (*A HWF
Anthology*)

Also by Tish Thawer Cont'd

The Rose Trilogy
Scent of a White Rose - Book 1
Roses & Thorns - Book 1.5
Blood of a Red Rose - Book 2
Death of a Black Rose - Book 3
The Rose Trilogy – 10th Anniversary Edition

The Ovialell Series
Aradia Awakens - Book 1
Dark Seeds - Novella (Book 1.5)
Prophecy's Child - Companion
The Rise of Rae - Companion
Shay and the Box of Nye - Companion
Behind the Veil - Omnibus

Stand-Alones
Guiding Gaia
Handler
Moon Kissed
Dance With Me
Magical Journal & Planner (non-fiction)

Anthologies
The Monster Ball: Year 3
Fairy Tale Confessions
Losing It: A Collection of V-Cards
Christmas Lites II

Ready for another adventure?

Turn the page for an excerpt from

Guiding Gaia

a YA fantasy standalone

PROLOGUE

*S*creams *pierced the air, but I kept swinging my sword. Souls of the damned swarmed the field, released from their fiery home in an attempt to keep me from achieving my goal. But after years of training, I was ready. Dropping to the ground, I spun in a circle with a wide sweep of my weapon, slicing through five at a time. Scorched earth crackled beneath my feet, dry and brittle as I slayed the next one.*

"No matter how strong you become, you will not succeed," a deep voice reverberated from behind me, clearing the field with his godly presence alone.

"Are you here to stop me?" My long, dark hair blew across my face, hopefully hiding the fear elicited by his words.

"No. But I am here to punish you." Lightning coursed between his fingers.

"Punish me?" I stood with my sword propped against the curve of my hip, its hilt heavy in my hand as the tip sank deeper into the ground.

"Look around, my darling. In your desperate attempt to save your daughter, you've neglected your duties, and the world has fallen into chaos because of you."

Taken aback, I raised my eyes to the horizon. Fires raged in the distance, their sparking fingers reaching into the churning sky. Violent clouds rolled, filled with lightning and ill intent. It was as if the sky and the earth were reaching for one another, determined to explode together, destroying everything in one final embrace.

"It will be up to you to guide the only one who can fix this. For that is your punishment, and the only way to secure a deal to save the one you love."

ONE

~ Varanasi, India ~

Rain pounded against the hotel windows, jolting me from the nightmare of my reoccurring memory, the force almost cracking the stained-glass as another monsoon raged outside. "Gaia, please. You need to calm down," I pleaded with the young goddess now under my care.

"I know, but it hurts."

"What hurts, honey?" I ran a hand down her auburn hair, offering comfort as if she was my own daughter—a habit we'd slid into over these last four months since our return to Earth.

"My blood. It feels like it's flowing the wrong way in my veins. It pushes and pulls." Gaia sank onto the gold duvet of the four-poster bed, dragging the heel of her hand back and forth along her forearm. "I need to get out of here." Her eyes snapped to mine as another wave of the unnatural storm thundered against the windows, their arches highlighted in sharp contrast by a kaleidoscope of colors reflected against the wall.

I didn't question her request. If Gaia needed to go, we'd go. Unfortunately, until we reached our destination here, we couldn't leave this portion of the world just yet. "I'll arrange transport to the final town on the map, but it is the middle of the night, so I'm not sure how easy that will be. It's unlikely the concierge will drive us himself." I set our bags near the door, then pulled my long, dark hair into a ponytail at the nape of my neck, knowing the storm wouldn't be the only thing I'd have to face outside.

"Fine. I don't care, just get me out of here, Demi."

The thin glass of the window shattered as the storm reached its peak, soaking the cream, patterned carpet and the antique wood furniture filling the room. Three hanging, multicolored lanterns crashed to the floor, extinguishing the candles the moment they fell. At this point, I couldn't tell if Gaia was upset because of the storm or if the storm was upset because of her.

Desperate to fulfill the oath of protecting my charge, I raced into the hall, the heels of my boots digging into the carpet as I dodged silver trays of discarded dishes lining the floor. Sharp scents of curry and chai permeated the air as I pushed into the stairwell and jumped over the edge. I dropped three floors in a single leap, straightening just in time to see a group of men heading straight for me.

The Crags were here.

Two months after Gaia's rebirth and our return to Earth, they cornered me in the dark alley between the hotel and the restaurant Gaia had started to favor. Pizzeria Vaatika Café sat minutes from the Ganges, but was now underwater, as the river had flooded and overflowed its banks just three days ago. They offered some of the best pizza and banana honey pancakes I'd ever tasted, but on the night of the attack, our takeout ended up on the ground while I battled the *men* sent to stop us. Seven continents, seven treasures of Gaia, all placed in sacred spots around the world at the time of creation—it was our mission to retrieve them, and the only way to save Earth from destruction ... or from Gaia herself.

Smashing through the hotel side-door, three Crags rushed inside. While they resembled human men in their current form, their lumbering movements and lanky limbs told another story. I reached into the folds of my black leather trench coat and unsheathed my sword from its magically hidden pocket. Metal clanged while they tried to best me, my muscles tensing as two more poured through the battered opening—all determined to reach the goddess three stories above our heads.

"Not gonna happen, boys." I rushed forward into the onslaught, matching their strikes, blow for blow. Blood rained down, coating the white tile floor in the darkened stairwell as the Crags scrambled to escape my wrath. After slicing through the stomach of the nearest man, I turned to see the final one slip past me, his red eyes glowing in triumph as he raced up the stairs.

"She's mine now, bitch," he snarled.

I crouched down, pushed off the ground, and flew into the air, snagging the handrail above me. Before he could reach the second floor, I flipped into his path. One swipe through his neck, and Gaia was safe again ... for now.

The wind howled through the broken glass below, reminding me of the task at hand—transportation out of here. I dropped back to the main level, my boots hitting the floor with a thud. Stepping over what remained of the Crags, I was happy to see their bodies disintegrated already. Minding the protruding glass of the shattered door, I crept out into the storm and smiled. The bad guys drove a nice car.

Rushing back inside, I toed through the Crags' remains until I found a set of keys lying in the dust. *Score.* With all the elements of our escape in place, I raced back upstairs, concealing my sword again before reentering the room.

"Let's go," I shouted, grabbing our bags from the floor.

Gaia looked up, her green eyes pinched in pain. "What happened? What took you so long?"

"Nothing happened. It just took a minute to arrange our rental." I looked to the floor, drawing attention to the drips of water falling from my drenched hair. "And as you may have noticed, it's a little wet outside," I teased—my usual attempt to hide anything was wrong.

"I'm aware." Lightning streaked across the sky, backlighting the eighteen-year-old goddess as she stood silhouetted against the maelstrom outside. Her auburn hair was wind-whipped and plastered to her neck and face, and though newly reborn, her divinity was something she could never hide … at least not from me.

"How far is it to the temple?" she asked.

"Five hours, but hopefully, you can get some sleep along the way. You'll need your energy for when we arrive."

Gaia pulled her jean jacket over her soaked cotton tee and followed me from the room. She was oblivious of the Crags and their intent to kill her, and it was my job—and part of my punishment—to keep it that way. To protect her from everything ... even knowing they exist.

After losing my own daughter, and the training I forced myself through to try to get her back, this was a task I would not fail again.

TWO

Hues of pink and orange sliced across the horizon, the colors bleeding into the early morning sky. We would reach the Mahabodhi Temple in just over an hour. Located in the Bodh Gaya area of Bihar, India, it was a mecca for tourists, welcoming visitors from all over the world for well over two-thousand years. However, for our purpose, we'd be forced to sneak in before anyone here had a chance to wake.

"Hey, where are we?" Gaia looked out the passenger side window of the Crags' black Jaguar, her voice groggy with sleep but much more even than it had been during the storm.

"Just outside of Gaya City. We're almost there. Are you ready?"

"Yes, I think so. I feel much better. Thank you for getting me out of there, D."

"Of course. It's my honor and duty."

"Come on, Demi. Stop with that shit already. I get that you were sent here with me—bound to protect me or whatever—but we're more than that, right? I wouldn't want to be on this quest with anyone else." The young goddess grinned, a sweet smile lighting up her face.

"Yes, Gaia, we're more than that." My heart clenched in my chest.

Our initial four months were hard. The dynamics of bringing back a goddess beyond her own will required a certain amount of *cosmic* interference—hence her being reborn a teenager instead of simply awakened as the true goddess she was. With myself an eternal thirty-five, I'd been able to witness the world throughout the centuries. However, the moment she awoke, we were deposited on Earth together, and found Gaia's powers and memories to be limited, forcing her to learn all she could about the modern world and its customs today. Luckily, money wasn't an issue, as I'd been divinely gifted a limitless amount in the form of a little, black charge card I'd been putting to good use. But no amount of computers, books, or even the iPod I bought her could negate the frustration of being cooped up in a hotel for four months while learning to ease her way back into a world she, herself, had created. Hence the random storms due to her emotional outbursts.

How could the gods put something like this on a teenager? I rubbed a hand over my face. "Honey, I know things haven't been easy, but I'm truly honored to serve as your guardian, and it's not something I take lightly."

"Ugh ... you're always so uptight." Laughing, she turned back to the dark-tinted window, her red hair shining in the soft morning light. "It's so beautiful here."

I took a quiet breath, swallowing my sigh. Watching her process this world anew was often a heart-breaking task. She was the ancestral mother of all life, consort to Uranus—the creator of the heavens and the sky, and mother to the Titans themselves. She created all we see and know, and was now tasked to evaluate the chaos that enveloped that same world, deciding if it was worth saving or not. So far, I couldn't tell which way she was leaning. It would take us completing our mission before she regained her full powers and all of her original memories—both of which she'd need to make her final decision. So, in times like these, when she still noticed the beauty around her ... I took note.

"With this being our first stop, why don't you tell me all you've learned about the temple," I prompted. The world had changed so much since Gaia buried her treasures; recon and research had become a significant part of our mission.

"The temple itself is a straight-sided pyramid with a round stupa on top." Gaia broke into her Wikipedia, internet voice. "The main shikhara tower is over one hundred and eighty feet high, with smaller ones surrounding its base. The construction is typical Hindu architecture, originally made from bricks covered in stucco. The towers rise into the sky like mountain peaks, which is the literal translation of the Sanskrit word shikhara, that's used to describe the style."

I laughed. "Good. Now tell me about the interior and the history of the site."

"Siddhartha Gautama was a philosopher, medicant, meditator, a spiritual and religious leader in the 5th to 4th century BCE, and is revered as the founder of the world religion of Buddhism. As a young prince, he saw the world's suffering and wanted to end it, and found himself wandering the forested banks of the Phalgu River.

That's where he sat in meditation under the Bodhi tree for three days and three nights, and achieved enlightenment and the title of the Buddha after finding the answers he was searching for. After his awakening, he spent seven weeks at different spots in the vicinity, which are now all marked in specific ways." Gaia paused for a moment, counting on her fingers.

"The spot where he achieved enlightenment and spent the first week under the Bodhi tree is where the temple was built, with the sacred tree still inside." She cast an ornery look in my direction. "And we both know why he was drawn to that spot, right?" She lifted her hands and pointed both thumbs at her chest.

"Yes, Gaia, I'm fully aware your treasures are what made all of these sites special to begin with." I chuckled. "Now please, continue," I urged her on.

"Fine." She faked a huff and turned back to the window. "During the second week, it's told that the Buddha remained standing, uninterrupted and unblinking, staring at the Bodhi tree from a spot on a hill to the northeast. That spot is now marked by the Animesholcha stupa—the 'unblinking Buddha shrine'." She looked over her shoulder at me. "My favorite thing is how lotus flowers sprung up along the path he walked between the two locations. It's now called Ratnachakrama, or the jewel walk."

I glanced over, noticing a spark in her eyes.

"I hope we get to see that part." She turned back to the window, the longing on her face reflected in the glass.

"Me too. It does sound lovely."

"During the third week, though, things got hinky."

"How so?"

"The Buddha saw through his third eye that the devas in heaven weren't sure if he'd attained enlightenment or not. So, to prove himself, he created a golden bridge in the air and walked up and down it for the rest of the week."

I burst out laughing. "Wow, I guess that showed them."

"Absolutely. He then spent the fourth week near Ratnagar Chitya to the northeast, sitting inside of a beautiful, jeweled chamber he created, where he meditated on what came to be known as his 'Detailed Teachings'. It's said his mind and body were so purified that six rays of light burst from within him. Yellow for holiness, white for purity, blue for confidence, red for wisdom, and orange for desirelessness, with the combination of them representing the sixth and the whole of his noble qualities."

"That's incredible."

"I know, right? This has been one of my favorite sites to research," she continued. "On the fifth week, he answered questions of the Brahmins under the Ajapala Nigodh tree. That's the spot where the Buddha stated that people were not born as Brahmins, but their work defines them as one. There's a pillar there which marks the spot where he sat. During the sixth week, Buddha meditated by the lotus pond, then rested under the Rajyatna tree for the seventh, which is outside and behind the temple. Some say it's even more beautiful than the Bodhi tree itself."

Gaia fell quiet as we entered the complex, her focus solely on the massive temple looming straight ahead. Its imposing figure dwarfed any description ever written. Even pictures couldn't do it justice. There was no way to adequately describe its beauty or notate the spiritual energy radiating from its sheer presence without standing in front of it yourself.

I pulled the car to a stop in the deep shadow of a giant banyan tree, cut the engine, and slid out of the seat. With my senses on high alert, I did a quick sweep to make sure we were alone, then rapped on the window for Gaia to exit the vehicle.

"Do you know what to do?"

"I think so. I can feel it … here." She placed her hand over her heart and shuffled toward the entrance as if being pulled inside by an invisible cord.

I followed closely behind, scanning our surroundings with every step. Other small structures, beautiful in their own right, lined the main thoroughfare. Detailed carvings slinked up and around the curved pillars and square columns like snakes carrying secret messages to the gods upon their etched backs.

Nearing the main temple's large door, Gaia stopped and looked up, taking in its full expanse. The carved wooden entrance was over ten feet tall and held caricatures and symbols—none of which I could decipher, but Gaia could.

"The world has changed so much," she whispered, turning back to me with tears in her eyes.

"It has, but isn't that why we're here?" I gave her an encouraging nod, then turned around and prepared myself to guard the temple while she ventured inside. I had no doubt more Crags were bound to rear their ugly heads. "I'll be here, making sure you remain alone, but if you need me, simply call out."

Gaia took a deep breath, then opened the door and disappeared inside. I caught a glimpse of the large Golden Buddha at the front of the sacred space right before the door clicked shut between us.

The sound of bells rang out in the distance, and I looked over the wall to the nearest hill sloping away from the complex. A group of monks in orange robes all knelt upon individual prayer rugs, their vibrant colors lighting up against the green grass under the early morning sun.

I felt my body relax as their monotone chants reached my ears. Closing my eyes, I let their ritual wash over me, stunned into a reverent state as I thought about where I was.

Assigned to protect the goddess here on Earth, I still couldn't believe I was actually here … a witness to it all. The scent of fragrant blooms of jasmine and parijat reached my nose, once again awaking in me a deep-seated guilt. However, as their chants died away, a thick silence descended, heavy and unnatural.

The Crags had arrived.

Pulling my focus back to the complex, I knew they couldn't enter the sacred space. Protected by her treasures, the sanctuaries were impenetrable to the Crags. Yet, as soon as she stepped outside, they'd seek to claim her prize and wouldn't hesitate to destroy her in the process.

Sliding my sword from its hiding place, I crouched low and prepared for their attack, but nothing happened. Darkness wavered in the shadows of the trees, yet no one made a move. Then again, it wasn't me they were after.

Easing behind the nearest column, I squinted to locate the heart of the threat and spotted them in the trees. Six Crags hovered above our car—perched in the branches like jaguars themselves.

After re-sheathing my sword, I unhooked the custom bow from my back and aimed triple arrows in their direction instead. Singing through the air, my arrows hit their targets—disintegrating the first three Crags into dust. The other three dropped from the tree in a panic and began their retreat, only making it a few steps before another volley pierced each of their hearts.

Scanning the area again, I found no further threats and quickly stowed my bow. I moved back into position to await Gaia's return, and moments later, the heavy door creaked open, revealing the goddess with a burlap bag grasped tightly in her hand.

"Any problems?"

"No. Its energy was clear and pulled me to the exact spot where I left it. Granted, I had to destroy a few tiles and a section of the base surrounding the tree, but once inside, it was smooth sailing." Smiling, she lifted the bag. "And don't worry, I repaired all the damage. The sacred site remains exactly as it was."

"Good. Now let's get out of here before anyone shows up."

CPSIA information can be obtained
at www.ICGtesting.com
Printed in the USA
LVHW041624071222
734760LV00024B/761/J